Trail to Nowhere

Sheldon B. Cole

A Black Horse Western

ROBERT HALE

First published by Cleveland Publishing Co. Pty Ltd,
New South Wales, Australia
First published in 1967
© 2020 Mike Stotter and David Whitehead

This edition © The Crowood Press, 2020

ISBN 978-0-7198-3102-7

The Crowood Press
The Stable Block
Crowood Lane
Ramsbury
Marlborough
Wiltshire SN8 2HR

www.bhwesterns.com

Robert Hale is an imprint
of The Crowood Press

Typeset by
Derek Doyle & Associates, Shaw Heath
Printed and bound in Great Britain by
4Bind Ltd, Stevenage, SG1 2XT

ONE

DUST AND DISTANCE

All the anger that a fifteen-year-old boy can muster stabbed at the core of Jesse Gray as he kicked the mare along. A mile back he'd seen how the fence wire enclosing his mother's mean little property had been bellied out and broken so two calves could be forced through. Now he followed the signs of the calves plus a trio of horses.

Three horses. Three men. Jesse reined up the mare. Suddenly his freckled face looked older, strained. His wiry body was tight and tense and he could feel a nerve jumping in his jaw. Three men.

Maybe he should ride to town and tell the sheriff. After all, it was the sheriff's job to go after rustlers.

Jesse bristled. Why go for help? He wasn't just a boy. He'd been looking after the cattle and the chores ever since his father died six months ago, hadn't he? Well, he'd done some growing up in that time. As for the calves, they were the future, and he couldn't run away from that.

He kicked at the ribs of the mare and moved off. He knew he had to be careful; but, more important, he had to get those calves back. When they were born, just hours apart, he'd been man-proud ... and he'd never forget the look in his mother's eyes at the sight of the calf heifers fighting to their feet. He had felt her pride in him at that moment and it was a good feeling. But there were times when he'd seen something else in her eyes as she stared at him. Doubt. Well, it wasn't easy for her. No husband, the parched land, the miserable little herd of cattle, the debts

She was afraid. As this thought struck Jesse, fingers of fear clutched at his stomach. He jerked back on the reins and the mare pulled to a stop. What if his ma knew what he was doing now? She wouldn't want him to go on with it, that's what.

'Son, a man keeps what he's big enough to hold . . .'

His father's words repeated themselves in his brain. Funny. His father had said many things to him, but he remembered only that.

The track ran straight ahead before disappearing over a rise some few hundred yards distant. Jesse clucked his tongue and the mare moved along at a walk. Maybe the three men had too big a start on him, he thought. If they had already reached Box C land, that would be the end of it. He couldn't track men over the Box C – Jesse knew that hardcase Gus Cowley, owner of the spread, wouldn't take kindly to such a thing. So, if he reached Cowley range without overtaking the men who'd stolen the calves, he'd just have to turn around and go home. Then no one would be able to lay blame on him for the loss of the calves.

The tracks definitely led towards the meandering creek bed. The men would follow the creek north for sure. Jesse looked up. He could climb into timberland and save a few miles. He brought his feet forward in the stirrups, ready to kick back. All at once the cold hand of fear clutched harder at his innards. He didn't have a gun, he reminded himself. Without a gun, what could he say to the three men? Yet he knew he had to go on or the calves would be lost forever. Besides, if he turned away now, could he ever again feel the pride of being a man?

Decision made, he brought his heels back hard. The mare squealed in surprised protest, then brought her rear down and plunged ahead. Jesse jerked rein and the mare turned sharply and climbed up to timberland and then along a narrow trail. Finally Jesse came to an open place from where he could see the winding creek bed below and, far ahead, Box C fence. He sucked in his breath. Hardly half a mile away were the two calves being pushed along by three riders.

The boy looked at the riders, his squinting blue eyes recognizing each one. They were Box C hands. Sully Benjamin, big and fat and sloppy, never clean and sitting his horse now like a greasy hunk of lard; Will Pearl, lean as a beanpole, good with a gun and proud of it; and Arch Briller, a sullen-tempered brute of a man who seldom spoke and whose eyes were always cold and penetratingly cruel.

Something like a moan escaped from Jesse's throat as he kicked savagely at the mare's flanks. He just couldn't let them take the calves – had to do all in his power to get them back. The mare went into a hard gallop and travel wind whipped back the brim of the boy's tattered hat and entered his wide-open mouth.

The three men turned at the sound of pounding hoofs and reined up to watch, curiously, as the boy sent the mare down the slope to the flat and over the creek bed. Jesse reined up hard and the mare reared, sending fore hoofs kicking at the sky. When the mare came down Jesse had to fight to hold his seat. The men still stared at him. Then Sully Benjamin showed crooked teeth in a smile.

'Well,' he said, 'look what we got here – young Jesse Gray.'

Jesse was angry and uncertain at the same time. The three grinned at him.

'You got some kind of trouble, Jesse, boy?' Pearl asked.

'Hell . . .' Jesse struggled to bring out the words. His mouth felt dry and raw. 'Them calves . . . they're my ma's.'

'How's that again about the calves?' Benjamin said gratingly.

'They're ours!'

Pearl laughed. 'Listen to the boy. We're walkin' back two calves that strayed from the Box C and here he is claimin' they're his.'

'They got our brand,' Jesse said, the words coming in a rush. 'That big G – it's there plain as day. I put the iron to 'em myself.'

The smile left Benjamin's mouth and his face went hard. 'Now, hold on, boy. A mistake is one thing, but accusin' men of rustlin' – well, that's somethin' else again.'

'They hang you for rustlin',' Pearl put in. 'You sayin' we oughta be hanged, boy?'

'I think maybe you better apologize real nice,' Benjamin said, his voice thin-edged.

'I – I ain't apologizin',' Jesse said. His throat seemed tight and he felt like he was choking. 'Them's our calves – they're branded clear.'

'Branded clear, eh?' Benjamin said coldly. 'Now is that so, boy?'

Jesse's gaze fell on the two calves. As he saw the sharply defined brand marks, anger lanced into him like a knife, cutting past the fear Benjamin's presence had put in his stomach.

'You got no right!' he gritted.

'No right!' Benjamin echoed. 'You're crazy, Jesse Gray. You think anybody's gonna listen to you? If you lost two calves, then you'd best be out lookin' for 'em instead of botherin' men goin' about their rightful business. Now you clear outa the way before I forget you're still wet behind the ears and stupid.'

'No!' Jesse turned the mare side-on to Sully Benjamin. 'I'm takin' them calves!'

Benjamin shifted in the saddle, and turned to Briller. 'Well, now, Arch, just listen to the kid mouthin' off at us. What do you reckon we oughta do about it?'

Briller smiled crookedly and shrugged. Then

10

saddle leather creaked as Benjamin turned to look at Pearl.

'You got any ideas, Will?'

Pearl sucked at his teeth and said, 'The kid's full of sass. He sours my guts.'

'Yeah.' Benjamin nodded. 'He sure does that, don't he?' The big man turned towards Jesse. The last trace of amusement had left Benjamin's bloated face. 'You sound real sure of yourself, son. Tell you what I'd do if I thought somebody was stealin' my calves . . . I'd just take 'em back.'

Jesse swallowed. 'Didn't say you were stealin' them.'

'Well now, that's a mite better,' Benjamin drawled.

'But they're still our calves,' Jesse added nervously. 'I – I'll just turn 'em back then and no harm done.'

Jesse urged the mare towards the grazing calves but suddenly Benjamin's big stallion was in the way.

'You say no harm done, boy?' Benjamin's lips thinned out and his eyes were glittering chinks. 'I don't see it like that. You're tryin' to take our property. These are strayed calves. Anybody knows that you can keep calves that wander onto your own range.'

'But this ain't Box C land,' Jesse protested.

Benjamin pointed a big finger. 'That's Box C fence.'

11

'We're outside the fence.'

'You lost your sense of direction,' Benjamin said. 'You're now on Box C range.'

'Yeah,' Pearl said. 'You're trespassin', kid. People get shot for that.'

None of this was true and it was obvious to Jesse that the three men knew it. They were smiling again, but there was something else in their eyes.

'Wheel around and ride off,' Benjamin said. He added, 'While you can.'

They weren't going to let him take the calves. They were determined to steal them. 'No!' Jesse cried. He straightened in the saddle. 'They're our calves and—'

He broke off to the clatter of hoofs, then turned towards Benjamin and saw the big man's rock of a fist coming at him. The punch landed on the side of Jesse's head and lifted him from the saddle. His feet slid from the stirrups and he fell to the side of the creek bank. Through the haze that was suddenly before his eyes he saw the mare step away, then he saw Benjamin dismount and the big man loomed over him, blotting out the sky.

'We got some stray calves,' Benjamin said. 'You let 'em get away from you so they're lawfully ours. Right, boy?'

The injustice of the whole business burned fury

through the boy. He placed his hands on the ground, fought himself erect and stood defiantly before Benjamin.

'You're thieves!' he cried out.

'Damn you!' Benjamin roared. 'You need some teachin'.'

Jesse tried to jerk his head away from the punch he saw coming but Benjamin's fist exploded against his jaw and he fell. There was no pain. The force of the blow had numbed him. He looked up and Benjamin's face danced in his blurred vision. There was only anger now. He tried to regain his feet, heard a grunted oath from Benjamin, saw the man's boot grow larger and larger and then there was a crashing blackness.

And nothing.

The world was shaking. Something cold hit Jesse's face. He opened his eyes, saw Pearl's narrow face. Pearl poured water into his palm from his canteen, flung the water into Jesse's eyes. Then Pearl was no longer there and Benjamin's face was close to his own. Benjamin had him by the shoulders, was shaking him.

'Say it, boy, say you was wrong!'

'Nothing's changed,' Jesse croaked out.

'Damn!' Benjamin let go of him, brought back his hand, hit Jesse a vicious blow across the cheek.

Blackness descended, moved away. There were clattering sounds, then Pearl's voice:

'Somebody might listen to him.'

'He can't prove nothin',' Benjamin said.

'There's one way to be sure.'

Then Pearl entered Jesse's field of vision. His six-gun descended almost into Jesse's face. There was the click of the hammer.

'Leave him be,' Benjamin snapped.

'He talks too much,' Pearl said.

'We ain't boy killers,' Benjamin said. 'Anyhow, he can't do us no harm.'

The six-gun was lifted away, but Pearl's voice came at Jesse:

'You watch it, boy. If this ain't the end of it, then the next time I see you I'll be lookin' at a man.'

Blake Durant worked his blue-black stallion, Sundown, across the barren country. A hot breeze that fanned his face, sent a wash of memories through his mind. Overhead a buzzard wheeled in wide, lonely circles. It was a section of country which drew him back into the eternity of his own loneliness, which made his mind discard all thoughts of time or place. There was just dust and distance and the ever-present urge to move on, to keep going.

Sundown stopped suddenly and lifted his proud

head, his eyes widening in their search of the dry creek ahead and his nostrils quivered in their search for the scent of water. Blake Durant laid a sympathetic hand on his mount's bluish head and stroked gently.

'Not yet, boy,' he muttered.

The horse's coat was so dark that the sunlight striking it gave the illusion that it was black, the satin-smooth black of the true midnight cayuse. Sundown's head went down and Blake Durant clucked his tongue, the horse responding as always to the only man who'd ever swung onto his back and managed to stay there. Horse and man made the long, dry trek along the high creek bank until the creek bed turned sharply to the south. Before Blake Durant was a sun-washed pocket of country that reminded him of another place – of somebody who belonged there. Louise Yerby. A mental image of her came to him. His mouth tightened and his stare narrowed. Instinctively his hand stole up to the golden bandanna about his neck ... once again he went back to that late afternoon, with the shade from the poplars thrown coolly from her father's porch ... the crowd of people, silent, shocked ... her mother, collapsed in her husband's arms ... the cowhand who brought the news. Everything was very distinct, sharp in detail, a scene that pained him more with each day that passed. Dead. Louise Yerby, dead . . .

Blake pulled the horse roughly to the left. Sundown shucked a shoulder in rebellion of the unjust treatment, but Blake kneed him on, saying:

'Nothing here, boy. We'll try the valley.'

He set the powerful horse into an even pace and struck off into the heat-shimmered distance. Craggy peaks rose into the sky a long way ahead. The desert was behind him now. Austere, forbidding country ran to the right, a stark contrast to the lush range he'd ridden from one month previously, leaving his younger brother, Luke, to work the place. Reliable, positive-thinking Luke who did not really understand but had asked no questions.

Morning gave way to noon and noon to afternoon and still none of the creeks held a hint of water. Stopping in the shade of dead locust trees, Blake Durant wet the silk bandanna and moistened Sundown's mouth with it. He drained the last drops from the canteen himself. The heat was oppressive now.

The afternoon was near spent and a cooler wind had come up when he finally topped a long rise and looked down into a narrow valley. At the far end was a small, wood slab ranch house with smoke coiling away from a brick chimney. Blake worked the horse into shade and let Sundown pick his own trail.

Sundown went directly for the house, ears pricked, gait eager. Ten minutes later they were on a barren clearing with the cabin only fifty feet away. Blake drew rein, removed his hat and ran long, leather-burned fingers through his yellow hair. His green-eyed stare went over the clearing, to the barn, the horse yards, the trough Sundown was staring thirstily at. Sundown nickered impatiently, shoulders lifting, sides sweat-slicked and head twisting away from the pull of the bridle. The trough was filled to the brim, the afternoon sun gleaming from its unruf-fled surface. Blake kept a tight hold on Sundown, saying, 'Wait, boy.'

A sound from inside the house drew Blake's atten-tion. The door came slowly ajar but no definite shape materialized. Blake was sure he was being watched. He let the horse walk on to the hitch rail, then he lowered the hat to his head and sat motionless, looking straight at the partly open door.

He kept his hands high up on the pommel of his saddle and braced himself for questions.

The door creaked fully open a moment later and a rifle poked out, its bearer following – a young woman with untidy red hair, small curls loose about the side of her grave face.

'Don't move, stranger.'

Blake nodded calmly and told her, 'We've come

17

up bench country, ma'am. Been going all day. Be obliged for water for myself and the horse.'

The young woman was still in the frame of the doorway, rifle held forward. Blake saw the wear of harsh years in her pretty, straight-featured face. Her uncertain stare was fixed hard on him. But Blake sensed no real animosity. This harsh country would breed distrust in anyone.

'There's a trough at the side of the house,' she said finally. 'Help yourself.'

Blake nodded again, then came out of the saddle. The woman's gun lifted and he saw her hands whiten under the pressure of her grip, saw, too, that her look sized him up fully with no opinion touching at the expressionless pattern of her features. He led the horse to the trough, cuffed a slight dusty film from the water's surface and let the horse nudge past him to drink. Blake stood beside Sundown and dusted down his glossy back before loosening the cinch. Then let the reins drop and pulled a tobacco pouch from his pocket. He had the cigarette rolled and was lighting it when she said from just behind him:

'The horse is tuckered out.'

He had not heard her come up, yet her voice did not startle him. Turning, he measured her with a calm look. She stood some twenty feet away, still firmly clasping the rifle.

18

'We've covered some hard country today,' he told her. Sundown lifted his head, water dripping from his mouth. The horse looked at her and went back to his drinking. When Sundown had had his fill, he moved to the side of the house and began to crop grass which sprouted up in a thick clump from ground watered by the trough's overflow. Blake pumped water for himself, drank and finally sank his head into the trough, coming up shaking like a terrier at a rag and drawing both hands down his sun baked cheeks.

The woman backed away a little towards the corner of the house. She still watched him warily as he said, 'How far to the next town, ma'am?'

She pointed with the barrel of the rifle past the front of the house. 'Crimson Falls is across the hills. Fifteen miles and not easy going. Figure four hours at least the way your horse is.'

Blake nodded his thanks, drank again and then took a canteen from Sundown's saddle and filled it. Returning to the horse, he hooked the canteen, tightened the cinch again, swung up and rode slowly past the young woman. 'Obliged to you, ma'am,' he said. She stepped back to let him pass and Blake saw indecision in her face. She had let the rifle muzzle lower until it pointed at the ground.

'Wait,' she said.

Blake looked at her and thought her cheeks red-dened a little under his gaze. But he allowed that it might have been just the way the sunlight suddenly caught the side of her face.

The young woman turned towards the forbidding crags in the distance and said, 'Some sections of the trail are dangerous. If you knew the country there'd be no trouble getting through, but not knowing it might cause the horse unnecessary hardship. If you like, there's oats in the barn and you could rest him a spell.'

This time Blake was sure of the blush his gaze brought. Her face still held a measure of reserve but her expression had softened. The woman fidgeted with the ribbon of her blouse and pushed a strand of hair from her brow.

'That'd be fine, ma'am,' he said. 'The horse has done me proud this far and I don't like to keep pushing him. I'm obliged to you.'

'It's little enough I'm offering,' she said, and moved back to the doorway of the house.

Blake came out of the saddle and led Sundown off. In the barn he unsaddled the horse, rubbed him down lightly and filled the feed box with fresh oats. Then he walked outside again and sat on the ground in the shade of the barn wall. He tipped his hat across his face and let the weariness of his body drag him into a deep sleep.

A sudden sound jolted him awake. Even while his eyes were opening and his mind digging for awareness of time and place, his right hand slashed down for his gun butt. His gun was clear and level when he shook his hat back out of his eyes.

The young woman, cloth-covered tray in hand, stepped back in alarm, almost dropping the tray. Blake's look went to her, the raw edges of caution still etched in his tanned features. Then his expression was bland again. He put up his gun.

'Sorry, ma'am.'

The young woman bit her lip. 'I . . . I shouldn't have startled you.' She extended the plate towards him, adding, 'It's nothing fancy, but we don't see many strangers.'

Blake pushed himself to his feet, muttered his thanks, and took the plate from her. The woman rubbed her hands as if embarrassed before retreating down the clearing. Blake saw her hesitate in the doorway and look back. Even across the heat-seared distance he could feel her curiosity and interest. He concluded she was both a sensible and careful woman.

TWO

A BOY'S PRIDE

It was close to dusk and long shadows had closed on the clearing when Blake led Sundown from the barn. The young woman came into the doorway, one hand raised to shade her eyes from the sun's glare. Blake removed his flop-brimmed hat and smoothed down his thick yellow hair, saying casually, 'Much obliged, ma'am. We'll find the going a lot easier now.'

'Just neighborly,' she said, color rising lightly in her face.

Blake stepped into the saddle and Sundown shifted impatiently under him and moved off a couple of steps before Blake could restrain him. He noticed that the woman was taking deeper stock of him now and at the same time he found himself weighing her carefully. A sharp twitch of pain drove through him when she turned slightly away and soft curls, recently combed, caressed a smooth cheek. He drew a ragged breath. Why did he think of Louise? The thoughtful look in her eyes when they stood close to each other . . . the rise and fall of her high bosom . . . the sweet, sweet smell of her. Blake's hand went to the yellow silk bandanna and he realized with a shock how much this woman was like Louise, even to the slightly tilted nose, the wide expressive mouth and the delicate neck. His fingers opened and closed on the bandanna.

Then he raked Sundown about and drove the painful thoughts from his mind. He looked at the distant hills and was glad he had a hard ride ahead of him.

'If you mean to travel the night, stranger,' the young woman called out, 'maybe you should take the valley trail. It's ten miles longer, but if time isn't important it will suit you better.'

Her voice had the same warm ring now that Louise's often had. He realized that he didn't know her name. Maybe it was best not to know.

'Time is nothing,' he said, ready to ride on But she spoke again, closer now:

'Crimson Falls is a big town and still on the grow.

It's very wild.'

Blake nodded acceptance of the information. Whatever Crimson Falls was, he didn't care. The woman's sudden willingness to talk disturbed him, yet he could not bring himself to depart abruptly. He wondered how much loneliness was in her life, if she had a man. He wondered, too, what kind of a man he was. Then he looked back at her, saw questions in her eyes and knew she was wondering about him. Her uplifted face showed no signs of embarrassment. It was almost as if she had made a decision about him, that she wanted him to stay a little longer.

Sundown was restless under him and Blake was suddenly glad of that. ' 'Bye,' he muttered.

'Goodbye,' she said, and he saw her draw in a light breath which swelled her bosom. Her deep-set eyes settled calmly on him, as Louise's always had when she was sure of herself and could accept the waiting. He nudged Sundown forward and through the corner of his eye saw her walk back towards the house. Loneliness settled about him again. He worked his neck and felt the silky comfort of the yellow bandanna on his weathered skin. Then he kicked Sundown into a gallop and the horse, strength restored with grass and water, responded eagerly.

Blake was a hundred yards or so up the clearing

when a horse burst into view from the flat country. He saw a boy low on the horse's back, slapping the reins wildly. Hoof thunder brought Sundown swinging suddenly to the right. Blake drew rein as the boy thundered past; he saw the youngster's bloodied shirt and bruised mouth. Blake turned and watched horror rush into the woman's face, then he turned Sundown around and walked him back.

'Jesse, what happened?' the woman cried.

The boy reined in and jumped from the saddle. 'Ma, they stole our calves!'

'Who?'

'That polecat Benjamin and two of his friends.'

The woman grasped the boy's arms but he twisted free of her grip and started at a run for the house. She stood there, empty hands held out, face white with shock, tears glistened in her eyes. Then she looked imploringly at Blake and all at once he knew she had no one else to turn to.

Blake called, 'Hold on, son.'

The boy whipped about and glared at Blake, then turned to the woman.

'They stole our calves, Ma! I'm gettin' the gun and goin' back!' And he ran into the house.

Blake came out of the saddle. As he walked towards the woman he saw how fear had taken control of her. Then the door opened and Jesse came running from the house with a Winchester in his left hand. Blake stepped in front of the boy and whipped the rifle from his grip. The boy, jerked off balance, staggered a few paces before he swung around, a wild light in his eyes.

'Give it here, damn you! Who're you to buy in? I gotta have that gun and go back!'

'Simmer down and take it slow,' Blake advised.

But the boy made a lunge for the rifle. Blake lifted the gun high and pushed the boy off with his free hand. Then the woman stood between them, tears coursing down her cheeks.

'Jesse, listen to me,' she implored. 'I don't want you to take up a gun. It doesn't matter what happened; I won't see you killed like your father was.'

'I'm goin' back!' Jesse cried. 'I'm gonna shoot dead all three of 'em!'

'Ease down, boy,' Blake said gently. 'Nothing's so bad that it can't be put right.'

The youngster's face twisted. 'Who says so? They ain't your calves and you ain't been beat up like I was. Now you get the hell away and leave us be and let me have my gun.'

'Don't you want some help?'

The boy blinked his eyes, obviously surprised by the offer. The woman stepped close to her son and put a hand on his shoulder. Blake, watching while the boy trembled against the fury inside himself, was relieved to see the youngster's breathing grow less labored.

'Tell me what happened,' the woman said.

'It was the Cowley bunch, Ma.' Jesse shifted from his mother's grip. 'Sully Benjamin and that Pearl and Briller who always ride with him. They stole our calves and beat the hell outa me. No matter about that, though – I'm goin' back and I'm gonna kill him.'

Blake watched the woman's face go pale. Fear stiffened her lips and her body sagged. Then, in a voice so low that Blake had trouble making out the words, she said:

'I can't let you do that, Jesse. I won't let you. You're all I've got left.'

'Got to, Ma,' the boy said firmly.

Blake inspected the rifle. It was old, with a loose stock and a slightly rusted barrel. He moved away from the wall, drawing Jesse's stare. Man and boy studied each other, then the youngster said bitterly:

'What do you reckon I should do, mister, let them take our calves which was branded plain?'

'Before I answer a question like that,' Blake said, 'I'd like to hear the full story.'

Jesse glanced at his mother before saying, 'I came across 'em leading off two of our calves. I wanted 'em

27

back. They beat me up and told me to git. I didn't have no gun or nothin' and there was three of 'em.'

'No mistake about whose calves they were, eh?' Blake said.

'No mistake. We got few enough as it is. I know every head we got; branded 'em myself.'

Blake threw a look at the young woman and saw the glint of hope in her eyes. Then Jesse walked up to Blake, grim determination in his young face.

'I'm goin', mister, and nobody's gonna stop me – you, Ma, nobody. So hand it over.'

The woman, mouth pinched, pulled Jesse around. 'Listen to me, son, for heaven's sake. Those men will kill you. What will I do then? Please – forget about the calves and come inside and let me fix your face. Then we'll have a hot dinner and talk it over. In the morning perhaps we'll go into town, see Sheriff Dowd and let the law look into the matter.'

Jesse drew away, anger bright in his eyes. 'No. We let 'em get away with this and we might as well pack and git out. Don't worry, I'll be careful. I ain't no fool and I know what pa would've done and how he'd've done it.'

Blake looked at the woman's troubled face and felt sympathy tug at him. But he had feeling for this boy, too – a boy trying to be a man. Suddenly he made up his mind for both mother and son. He tossed the rifle to the youngster.

'You see me down to the valley trail, Jesse, so I won't lose my way.'

Jesse had caught the rifle. Now, after a searching look at Blake Durant, he tightened his belt and said, 'I got to go, Ma, I just got to.'

Jesse turned deliberately and mounted the mare. Blake caught up Sundown's reins and swung into the saddle. He circled back past the young woman and said, quietly, 'I'll be with him.'

Her eyes opened wide with uncertainty, but under the calm look of the stranger she drew in a deep breath and slowly nodded. Blake moved alongside the boy and then boy and man kicked their mounts into full gallop.

Dusk had settled in and the air was cooler. The blood had dried on the boy's face and he scratched some of it off, his fingers moving gingerly over the bruises. At the bottom of the valley, Blake drew level with Jesse. He sat easily in the saddle, the wind flapping his loose hide coat against his wide-shouldered, deep-chested body.

Blake's stare searched ahead. 'How far?'

'Ain't far. Just ahead down the creek was where I seen 'em. I'll track 'em down before dark sets in.'

'When you do, it might help to ask for the calves

29

again, Jesse. Could be they got you wrong last time.'

Jesse's eyes fired with annoyance. 'They didn't get me wrong, mister. They knew what they was up to – stealin', sure as hell.'

'You'll have company this time,' Blake said. 'Listen to me. Put it to them quiet, and keep that gun down.'

Blake watched the struggle in the boy's face. He wanted the boy to make the decisions. Jesse again wiped sweat from his face.

'You comin' along, mister?'

'Don't see how it will hurt any,' Blake said. 'Rustling is a hanging offence where I come from, but a man has to make dead sure of his facts before he lays a charge that serious. When we meet up with them, you ask and I'll listen.'

Jesse shifted uneasily in the saddle and Blake realized how young he was, how uncertain of himself – yet determined to prove himself and hang onto what was his. The man felt an immediate respect for the boy and nodded for him to proceed. Jesse let his mare pick her way through the fence and across the timbered slopes. Reaching the top of a rise, Blake looked to where Jesse pointed. Three men were squatted at the bend of the creek ahead, a fire's glow flickering bright across their sullen features.

Blake said, 'Go ahead, Jesse, and do your talking.'

Jesse gulped, touched the stock of the rifle, then

drew in a deep breath. Blake trailed the boy to the end of the slope where a big man stirred and looked up at them. He was chewing on fresh-cooked meat while he brushed bothersome flies from his face.

THREE

DRIFTER'S CALL

Sully Benjamin pushed himself off the rock's flat edge and hurled a partly chewed piece of meat into the leaf-flecked pool twenty yards away. He licked his fingers, wiped his mouth with his blood-stained sleeve and sucked his gums. Behind him the two men stopped eating and looked guardedly at Blake and the boy.

Blake's stare shifted from Benjamin and settled on a hung carcass, then onto a hide draped over a tree stump, beneath which the insides of the slain calf had been spilled and left for the flies to worry.

'They kilt one of 'em,' Jesse said at Blake's side, and leaned forward in the saddle, preparing to dismount. But Blake's hand went across his chest, holding him back.

'Take it easy, son,' Blake advised and moved into tree shade. The silence of the twilight hour was complete. Blake sized up the trio again and decided that the boy's earlier description fitted them perfectly. They looked rugged, sour-bellied, hardcase cowhands. 'Go down now,' Blake said, 'and do what I told you.'

Jesse needed no prompting. When he reached the bottom of the slope and the three grouped to confront him, Blake came a little closer. His lean, sun-baked face showed no emotion. Nor was there any hint of decision in his green eyes. He stared hard at the three men, drawing their attention away from the boy.

Sully Benjamin gestured with his left hand and shifted his right closer to his gun butt. 'Well now, what've we got here?' he drawled.

Jesse walked to where the carcass hung.

'Yours?' Blake asked.

Jesse nodded. His mauled face was white and his lips quivered.

'Yeah, ours right enough, mister. They butchered 'em!'

Blake let Sundown shift closer and his look hardened as it settled on the big man now leaning against a tree, left hand up-stretched, his right firmly planted on his gun butt. Grim curiosity was etched in his fat, grease-stained face.

'What's your business?' Benjamin asked sourly.

Will Pearl squatted at the edge of the creek, positioned, Blake knew, to get him in crossfire if trouble erupted. Pearl looked relaxed to the point of disdain. The third man Blake ignored; he seemed slow-moving, uncertain.

'The boy's laying a claim against you gents,' Blake said calmly.

'That so?' Sully Benjamin growled.

'He said you stole two of his ma's calves,' Blake went on easily. 'I guess the brand he's showing me right now proves he's right.'

Benjamin wiped his hands down his grubby shirt. His head didn't move but Blake saw his glance flick sideways at Will Pearl. Then the big man's jaw squared and his lips tightened.

'Mister,' Benjamin said, 'do you always listen to what kids tell you?'

'You stole 'em right enough, Benjamin,' Jesse said, waving the branded hide in Benjamin's face. Benjamin pursed his lips. Anger tightened his face.

'Boy, don't you know when to quit?' Benjamin said. As he spoke he moved to the left, letting Arch Briller get a clear view of Blake.

'You're a damn thief!' Jesse charged. 'And worse,

34

you ain't got no feelings. That calf wasn't even half grown and you slashed it open, killed it!'

Benjamin's eyes blazed. 'Boy, take a hold on your tongue or I'll bust you again.'

Blake Durant was no more than a few yards from Benjamin now. 'The boy won't be touched,' he said, and there was a ring of authority to his voice which made Benjamin's mouth gape open. Will Pearl started to rise, body stiff with tension, cold black eyes narrowing. Briller licked his lips and gulped. Jesse shifted across to where Blake Durant sat his horse.

'The brat's a damn liar, mister, not that I care what you think,' Benjamin snorted angrily. 'Now get to hell outa here and take the kid with you. We got no time to jaw with interferin' jaspers that jump right outa the ground.'

Blake smiled. 'You'll release the other calf and pay for the one you killed,' he said firmly.

'You loco?' Benjamin snapped.

Blake shook his head. 'Just being fair to the boy, mister.'

'Go to hell then, and go pronto!' Benjamin rasped. 'Me, I'm headin' home. Had a hard enough day as it is.'

'It could get harder,' Blake said tonelessly.

Benjamin's face went dark with rage. 'Mister, you got a head so choked with dust you can't understand a man when he speaks plain. I'm heading home – now!'

Pearl snickered and Briller began to sweat. Blake ignored them, concentrating only on Benjamin who had shown himself to be the leader of the trio.

'Pay the boy,' Blake said.

Pearl spoke for the first time. 'Mister, you're lightin' a fuse.'

Blake eyed him. 'If you're the fuse, start spluttering.'

'Damn you!' Pearl spat.

Blake saw the thin man's hand go for his gun butt. His own hand slashed down and he drew and fired. The bullet smashed Pearl's chest and sent him reeling, disbelief twisting at his face. Pearl fell almost at Sundown's fore hoofs.

Blake's gaze swung from the dead man and settled on Briller whose hand had also gone towards his gun butt. Briller jerked his hand away and shook his head. Blake's look shifted and he saw Benjamin detour his hand away from his gun butt and clamp it against his ribs.

'Sensible,' Blake told him, then he motioned Jesse forward and said, 'Get your calf while these two empty their pockets.'

Benjamin cursed under his breath and glared at Jesse as the boy hurried past. 'Why should we empty our pockets, mister?'

Blake watched the color die in Benjamin's face. He pointed to the hung carcass and told him, 'To pay for that.'

Benjamin gaped. 'Pay for that mangy yearling? You got to be funnin'.'

'Neither of us believe it's time for jokes, Benjamin,' Blake said. 'Empty your pockets and quick.'

'Go to hell and blazes, damn you!' Benjamin snapped.

Blake drew in an impatient breath. 'I've asked you once. That's my only count.'

Benjamin closed his mouth. Arch Briller, dead still, face bloated with fear, gulped uneasily and waited for Benjamin to lead the way. Finally, Benjamin growled, 'Arch, pay him.'

Briller scowled, felt around in his Levis pocket and brought out change. Blake saw a gold piece and said, 'Jesse, take the gold eagle and get on home.'

Jesse stepped to Briller and plucked the gold piece from his grimy hand. Then Jesse slapped the freed calf on the rump, sending it running, before he mounted the mare. He looked at Blake.

'You comin', mister? Ma'll be—'

'Get on home, Jesse,' Blake said. 'Go! Git!' He waited until the boy's mare reached full gallop before turning to Benjamin and Briller. 'Shed your guns. Throw them into the water back of you.'

Briller quickly disposed of his gun. Benjamin was a bit slower. When both guns had been swallowed by the creek water, Blake made Briller get rid of Pearl's gun, too.

'All right,' he said, 'pack your friend on his horse. Then head on, both of you.'

When Benjamin sat in the saddle again and Briller had Pearl's horse behind him, Blake said:

'You two are quittin' winners, even though you might not know it. Leave the boy and his mother be.'

Benjamin grunted a curse and kicked his horse into motion, Briller following. Blake went up the slope and holstered his gun. He kept his stare fixed on the two men, but he was too far from Sully Benjamin to hear the big man say:

'I'm gonna get him, no mistake. I'm gonna shoot his guts out.'

When the pair were out of sight, Blake worked his horse back down the creek and rode onto the widow's land. He saw Jesse a long way off. The boy, turning, waved, and he waved back. Then Blake went on his way, the cool night closing in on him and Sundown eagerly striding under him. Blake Durant was once more a man alone, on the drift.

*

Jessica Gray sat at the kitchen table in a hunched posture that made her look older than her years. She felt wretched. For half an hour she had been remembering how life, had been six months previously, when her husband was alive. She could hear him talking even now, seriously caught up in the life out here, so apprehensive at times and yet so excited at other times about their chances. She had always known him to be a man among men, and it was this more than any other thing that had made her accept his offer of marriage. There had been some wonderful moments, some which she would never forget, particularly when for the first time in her life she had known what older women had told her about, about becoming a woman, a full woman, alive and needed and able to give so much. Since he'd died there had been moments when she could easily have given up. That had been in the beginning of the loneliness, when she had to fight to appear brave in the eyes of her boy. Her sorrow was a constant thing and there was no getting away from it, however much she struggled against it.

When the sound of the single shot reached her, Jessica spun about, her hand going to her mouth to press back a cry. Then the echo of the shot was lost in the howling wind that banged the window shutters. She bit her lip, trying not to think that Jesse might be alone; she dared not think of that. The stranger had struck her as a man who offered himself, for a reason she did not understand. Somewhere, back in the dark reaches of her mind, she knew that he had not ridden on.

Jessica rose and moved restlessly about the room. From time to time she went to the doorway and looked hopefully across the clearing, desperate for a sight of Jesse riding home. She blamed herself for letting him go off on his own – but how could she have stopped him? There was too much of his father's stubbornness in him.

Dusk fled the clearing and night began to close in. Soon she could see no further than the hitch rail. What if Jesse did not come back? She shook her head and pushed the terrible thought away. There was nothing left but the boy; her life was for him. Going on would be impossible without him.

She lit the lantern, raked the fire, added fresh wood and set about getting dinner. That done, she walked in a half daze outside. Nothing helped. There was still the interminable waiting, the emptiness.

Then Jesse came out of the twilight, the calf running in front of him. Jessica held her hands to her bosom and fought down the emotions stirring inside her. Jesse brought the calf past her and called back:

'Everything's fine, Ma.'

Jessica looked down the clearing and saw that Jesse had returned alone. A moment later she heard him closing the yard gate and she called, 'Best wash up, dinner's ready.'

It was ten minutes before Jesse came into the house, his face washed clean of blood, making the bruises and cuts stand out clearly. He had combed his hair, brushed down his faded Levis and put on another shirt. Jessica put his meal down. 'Eat,' she said.

Jesse looked vaguely at her and plied himself to the food and all the time Jessica Gray kept away from her son, afraid of breaking down, so great was the relief of having him back. She wondered briefly about the stranger. Had he helped Jesse?'

Then Jesse said, 'Ma, I got twenty dollars for the other calf.' He put the gold coin on her side of the table. Jessica picked up the gold eagle and looked curiously at him.

'They'd killed one and was eatin' it, damn polecats,' Jesse said, as though eager to get the words out. 'Mr Durant, the stranger, he said it was fittin'. You can get that new dress now, Ma.'

Jessica stepped to her son and hugged his head against her bosom. Jesse pulled away, frowning. 'Aw, Ma, hell.'

'Is there shame in wanting to hold your son and be proud of him, Jesse?' she said. 'There's little enough we have.' She sat down and turned the coin over and over in her hand.

Now words came tumbling out of Jesse. 'We found Benjamin and Pearl and that sneaky no-good Briller at the creek, gorging themselves like the pigs they are. I went and asked 'em for the calves again, like Mr Durant said, but just as I figured they told me to go to blazes. Then Pearl went for his gun and Mr Durant shot him down. After that there weren't no more trouble. Benjamin just kinda folded up, and Briller, like I figured him all along, near died of fright.'

Jessica dropped the gold coin onto the table and pulled back from it, as though it had blood on it. She looked horrified at her son, shocked by his ready acceptance of the killing of a man. She had seen her husband kill a man who had come riding roughshod through their place while she was carrying Jesse. Then Chad had withdrawn into himself, saddened by the loss of a man's life, no matter how justly he had acted. But Jesse seemed to be excited, almost triumphant.

She was reaching for words to combat Jesse's attitude when he went on, grinning boyishly, 'I don't reckon we'll have no more trouble with them Cowley

42

jaspers, Ma. They'll leave us alone, you'll see, so you got nothin' more to worry about.'

'Nothing to worry about?' Jessica snapped at him. 'A man dead?'

'Took our calves and wouldn't give them back, Ma,' Jesse said hotly. 'Anyhow, it was Pearl who forced the play and got what he deserved.'

'Jesse!' The name exploded from Jessica. Then she shook her head, unable to cope with her son's new-found disregard of life. 'What are you saying? Do you think a man's life is less important than a calf's?'

'Depends on who the man is, Ma,' Jesse asserted firmly. 'Bein' Will Pearl, I reckon it's about even.'

Jessica could not believe her ears. She stared at the coin on the table and felt a chill run through her body. She remembered what an arresting figure the stranger had appeared to be, with his wide shoulders, deep chest and range-hard body, slimming down to a sinewy waist. She saw again the lean, deeply tanned features and green eyes – eyes which had stirred half-forgotten emotions in her body. She shuddered, remembering how he had drawn his gun at the sound of her approach to him – one minute asleep, the next alert, gun lifted, finger white on the trigger, ready to kill.

'I won't have you talking like that,' she said. 'A man's life is important. It doesn't matter who the

43

man is – it's not your right to sit in judgment on him and mete out punishment for anything he may have done. We have the law for that, and as long as you live here with me, you'll be guided by the law and not by the actions of a stranger, no matter how charitably he acted on our behalf.'

Jesse looked up sullenly as she rose, picked up the gold coin and put it in her apron pocket. Then, stepping away from her son, she said quietly:

'Finish your dinner. There's more tonight if you want it.'

Jessica busied herself in the kitchen again while the boy ate. When Jesse brought his plate in, his face was set in thoughtful lines. Seeing his uncertainty, she placed an arm around him and kissed him lightly on the forehead.

'It will be all right,' she told him. 'Get a good rest tonight.'

Jesse nodded and went to his room. When Jessica came in to check on him, he was asleep on his bed, fully dressed, right down to his scuffed boots. She smiled when she saw the innocence of his look and knew that, no matter what had happened that day, he was still a boy. She removed his boots, gave them a thorough polish and put them under the bed where he could get them easily in the morning. He needed another pair badly. As soon as she could spare the time, she thought, she would take him to town. Jessica pulled the single blanket over her son and tucked in the sides. Then she left his room and picked up her sewing basket.

Now her thoughts returned to Blake Durant. She was annoyed at herself for thinking harshly about him. He'd helped her son.

'May the Lord go with you,' she whispered.

FOUR

'KILL HIM!'

Gus Cowley sat on his front porch, a self-indulgent smile on his craggy face. It had been a good year for him, one of the best in the twenty years since he'd come to these parts. The ranch was running smoothly and his hired hands were a reliable bunch. One or two of them gave him trouble now and again but a little pressure soon brought them back into line. No, he told himself, things couldn't be much better, not since he had hired Jud Slater to handle his bigger troubles. Slater was a gunfighter, permanently sullen, mean as a rattler and a born killer. The right man, Gus Cowley agreed, in the right place.

Cowley stretched out, rubbing his right hand. Of

late he had been feeling pain in that fist, and he'd been meaning to ride to town and see Doc Sommers about it. But, with the roundup nearing, he had put the trip off. A secondary reason for deferring his trip was the restlessness in his men, natural enough because it was Cowley's habit to keep them confined to the ranch just before roundup so they'd be fit and in fine fettle for the hard work ahead. Later, after the cattle were sold off, he would let them hell it up any way they liked – but in town, not here.

In the coolness he retained his good mood, watching the hands move across the clearing from bunkhouse to cookhouse. Cowley felt like some hard drinking himself, but in deference to the limitations he had enforced on his men he denied himself the pleasure. He rose from the chair and walked stiffly across to the porch rail and drew in a heavy breath. I'm getting old, he told himself and stood against an overhang post, rubbing his hand up and down his shirt front.

Out of the gloom at the end of the clearing three shapes materialized. Sully Benjamin was in the lead, with Arch Briller behind him. The trailing third horse was riderless. Cowley straightened up. Pearl had ridden out with Benjamin and Briller to check the bottom country bordering on the Gray place.

The two riders came on. Cowley saw that Benjamin

was hesitant, not arriving in his usual blunt manner. He had no illusions about Benjamin's love for range work and was fully aware of Benjamin's habit of cleaning up early, putting his supper away and getting involved in a nightly card game with the bunkhouse fraternity.

Slowly the two men closed the gap and drew rein just short of the porch. Benjamin sat upright in the saddle, an unusual pose for him, and Briller looked more uncertain of himself than usual. Gus Cowley's gaze swung past them and came to rest on the figure draped across the saddle of the third horse. Cowley had seen enough dead men in his time to know that he was looking at one.

He straightened and ran a thick hand through thinning hair going gray at the temples. 'What the hell's this, Benjamin?' he growled.

Cowley saw the cowhand's face tighten, saw his jaw muscles work. Whatever it was, he knew Benjamin was sour about it.

'It's Will Pearl, Mr Cowley. He got shot.'

Cowley's eyes darkened and his mouth twitched. He grasped the porch rail and peered down angrily at the two men.

'How'd it happen, Benjamin, damn you?'

'We was jumped at the creek,' Benjamin said and looked bleakly at Briller, sharp warning in the glance.

'Jumped? Who the hell by? Who the hell had the nerve to jump my hands?'

Cowley's fierce look remained fixed on Benjamin, saw the uncertainty in the cowhand's black eyes.

'It was a damn tinhorn stranger,' Benjamin said. 'We come across two of the Gray calves strayin' on our range so we took 'em in tow.'

Cowley's face jolted under the pressure of his increasing anger. 'I told you to leave her be, damn you, Benjamin! I said to steer right clear of her, give her no reason to look for backing from anybody in these parts. By hell, if you—'

'They was strays and on our side of the fence,' Benjamin grated sourly. 'So we brought them along. What the hell did you want us to do, take 'em back to the woman and maybe lick her boy's boots?'

Cowley's heavy-featured face closed up. He rubbed a hand tiredly behind his neck, gave Briller a searching look and then growled, 'Get on with it.'

Sully Benjamin shifted in the saddle and Cowley knew he was bridling at having to explain the business. But the rancher meant to have full details and didn't give a damn if Benjamin never got supper, never got cleaned, never sat in a card game that night.

'Ain't nothin' much more to it,' Benjamin returned tightly. 'We was ridin' down the creek bed when the Gray kid come hollerin' down on top of us callin' us thieves. I give him a couple of cuffs to shut him up and then this stranger jumped up outa the ground. Will went for his gun but was beat to the shot and got kilt.'

Gus Cowley sucked in breath. He noticed Briller studying his hands thoughtfully and he had the feeling that Briller was keeping out of it on Benjamin's orders.

'What's your version, Briller?' Cowley asked, and the thick-set man stirred in the saddle, his sullen face clouding.

'Same as mine,' Benjamin said quickly.

A curse ripped out of Gus Cowley. 'I want to hear it from him so shut down, damn you!'

Benjamin grumbled under his breath and fixed Briller with a severe look. The big cowhand licked at his lips, drew in a quick gulp of breath and said nervously, 'What Sully says is right, Mr Cowley. We were jumped, didn't get a chance. This jasper just happened up, shot Will and then he wanted us to pay up for the other calf.'

'Other calf?' Cowley barked. 'What other calf? What the hell were you hellions doin' anyway?'

Sully Benjamin moved his horse about, scowling at Briller. Cowley, sensing Briller was the weakest link in this team, concentrated on him.

'Keep tellin' it,' Cowley said.

Briller went on hesitantly. 'The one we kilt and was gettin' some meat off, Mr Cowley. That was why we was beat to the draw. We didn't hardly hear 'em comin', then that Gray kid was yelling his head off.'

Cowley let out a muffled curse, pounded down the porch, went to Benjamin and yanked him down from the saddle. He hurled Benjamin against the porch and smashed a fist into his face. Benjamin rolled along the rail and struck his shoulder on an over-hang post. As Cowley came at him, Benjamin's hand clamped on his gun butt.

Cowley drew up short, his huge chest heaving, fists held at the ready. 'Do that, Benjamin, do it! Go on, damn you!'

Sully Benjamin stood frozen, his face working, burning anger in his black eyes. He held Cowley's testing look for a long moment, then he sighed and lifted his hand clear.

'You got no damn right to maul a man, Cowley,' he muttered.

'I got any right I like to take, Benjamin, and don't you ever forget it. Now we'll start all over again and Briller will do the tellin'. And, by hell, if you messed up things worse than I've heard so far, I'll kill you and have you buried alongside Pearl and good damn riddance!'

Benjamin wiped blood from his mouth and swayed away from Cowley. Then, face hidden in the dark near the porch overhang, he shot a bitter look Briller's way. Briller gulped and fumbled at the reins across the pommel of his saddle. His face was strained as his gaze shifted, from one man to the other.

'Tell me, damn you, mister!' Gus Cowley barked.

Briller nodded and wiped sweat from his face. 'Like Sully said, Mr Cowley, we was jumped. We was restin' after a hard day, figurin' to have us some fresh meat in the cool before bringin' what was left back to the boys as a treat. Then, after Will got gunned down, this here jasper told us to dig out our money. He took twenty dollars of mine and gave it to—'

'Twenty dollars? What in hell for, Cowley?'

'The calf, Mr Cowley, the one we butchered.'

Cowley's brows lifted to reveal the cold shock in his eyes. 'Twenty dollars for a yearling calf, mister? You loco?'

'That was this jasper's price.'

Cowley wheeled on Benjamin. 'A cowpoke and a snotty-nosed kid took you for twenty dollars Benjamin? You got a generous streak in you all of a sudden?'

Benjamin's mouth tightened but he said nothing. Cowley punched the porch rail and swore violently under his breath. Then he breathed in deeply, trying to get control of his temper. Succeeding in part, he swung back onto the porch but still regarded Sully Benjamin disdainfully.

'Okay, Briller, let's have the rest of it,' he said wearily. 'For what it's worth.'

Briller, appearing relieved at the change in Cowley's tone, said, 'Well, Mr Cowley, that was about it, 'cept this jasper made us throw away our guns and then put Will's body on his horse. After that he hit leather. The Gray kid had already gone home, takin' the other calf and my twenty dollars.'

Cowley shook his head in disgust and clapped both hands onto the rail. 'You're damn fools, both of you. Can't I take my eyes off any of you without you ride into trouble? I got to wet nurse you all the damn time?'

Benjamin stood beside his horse, eyes down. Briller sat rigidly still in the saddle.

Cowley shook his head slowly. 'So you locked horns with the Gray kid when I told you to leave him and his ma alone. Then you got Pearl shot and paid up twenty dollars for a yearling calf. That's great, just real great.' He moved about, scowling at Benjamin all the time. 'If I got twenty dollars for every calf on my range I could buy up a good slice of Texas.' He breathed in deeply again. 'Well, no matter now, it's done. But hear me out, Sully – you're ridin' close to the wind. I don't like slackers on my payroll. Briller, get a shovel and bury Pearl.'

Briller wasted no time pulling out, plainly glad to be on the move. Cowley then let Benjamin walk his horse off, but he sent some curses after him. He wondered if there would ever come a day when trouble of some kind was not on his doorstep. He went inside, studied the whisky cabinet thoughtfully for a moment then crossed to it and poured himself a double slug of whisky. He tossed the drink down in one gulp and relaxed as it warmed his insides.

Ten minutes later Sully Benjamin opened the door, leading a tall, lean man wearing double gunbelts. When Benjamin hesitated, the tall man brushed past him and came casually across the room. Benjamin turned to leave.

But Gus Cowley snapped, 'Keep comin', Benjamin. I ain't finished with you.'

The tall man went to the wall near the cabinet, moving with the effortless grace of a cat. He leaned against the wall, black eyes sleepy.

'Trouble?' Slater asked.

'Of a kind, Jud,' Cowley said. 'But nothin' we can't handle.' Cowley filled his glass a second time and then related Briller's story.

The tall man eyed Benjamin bemusedly and said,

'A kid and a drifter took you apart and hooked you for twenty dollars to boot?' His grin spread across his face, drawing deep grooves into the corner of his mouth and right down his lean, tanned cheeks.

'We was jumped, Slater,' Sully Benjamin muttered. 'You couldn't have done no better.'

'My paydirt against yours, Benjamin,' Jud Slater said, still grinning while he thumbed his hands under the shining buckle of his gunbelt.

Gus Cowley studied each of them coolly in turn before he gestured impatiently with his filled glass, and called, 'OK, OK. Let's not complicate the issue. Pearl's dead. Would have happened sooner or later the way he was always snortin' for trouble. What worries me is this driftin' jasper, Jud. If he's workin' for the Grays, they could be fixed to fight me off. I've got things sewn up with the bank and the Gray woman's only got a few weeks left before her time's up. Then I take over. Jud, what I'd like you to do is ride over there and take a look at the hand she hired.'

'Sure,' Slater returned, lifting his hands and flexing them. He straightened against the wall, his coarse shirt scratching noise from the bare boards. To Gus Cowley he looked as relaxed as a man could be.

'Be a waste of time goin' to the widow's place,'

Sully Benjamin put in. 'The kid headed home with his mangy calf but the tinhorn headed for town.'

'Tinhorn?' Jud Slater said. 'And you didn't take him?'

'Cut it, Jud!' Cowley said as Benjamin scowled darkly. 'Sully's had a hard day what with his friend Pearl shot down before his eyes.' Cowley walked to the door, opened it for Jud Slater and let him pass onto the porch. He leaned on the rail and stared into the darkness before he went on. 'It's town then, Jud. You know what to do, eh?'

Slater nodded, then jerked a thumb at Benjamin. 'He rides with me?'

'That's right,' Cowley said. 'Sully can point him out.' He paused. 'Just don't step on the law's toes, eh?'

'Not unless it can't be helped,' the gun-handler said.

Cowley roughed his hair and breathed out tiredly, 'Well, be careful. I've got the Gray business legally tied down, but I don't like the idea of a stranger ridin' in and killin' one of my men. See he gets the message about that. Understand?'

Jud Slater smiled faintly. 'Kill him?'

Cowley shrugged. 'Leave it to you. When you meet him, try to think of Will Pearl as one of my best men, as loyal as they come and, like Sully here, always thinkin' of the ranch first and himself second. A top hand, dead now, jumped by a drifter.'

Jud Slater nodded and went down the steps, walking with the easy manner of a man who had complete confidence in himself.

Cowley turned to Sully Benjamin. 'Ride into town with Jud and see if you can do something right for a change.'

Then Cowley wheeled about, stepped into the house and slammed the door in Benjamin's face. Benjamin spat a curse at the door before stepping off the porch and swinging onto his horse. While he waited for Jud Slater to come down from the stables, he let his horse pick its way along the barren clearing.

Cowley was having his third drink of the evening when Jud Slater came along the clearing and without a word to Sully Benjamin, worked ahead and let Benjamin eat his dust.

FIVE

CRIMSON FALLS

Blake Durant reached Crimson Falls three hours after leaving the Gray place. The going through the valley had been easy and Sundown, after his rest, had made good time, getting skittish only once, when they passed a group of corralled mares. Durant himself was bone-tired and in need of a drink, so he hitched up in front of a mid-town saloon and stepped through paint-faded batwings into a garishly lighted big room packed with cowpokes, gamblers, ranchers, townsmen, itinerants. The sudden noise was thunderous. He took a quick look around. It was the kind of a crowd which could, in a blink, erupt into a brawling, knuckle-crunching melee.

Durant edged himself between an argumentative group of cowpokes and dropped loose change on the counter. The barkeep, bushy-browed and sweating, hustled about urgently. The smell in the room was of men's sweat, spilled whisky, dirty sawdust and tobacco smoke. The hanging lanterns gleamed yellow through the screen of smoke and gave the occupants of the room a vagueness which suited Durant.

In answer to the barkeep's uplifted eyebrows, Blake said, 'Rye.'

He tossed the drink down before the barkeep had collected the price for it, pushed the glass forward. 'The same.'

The barkeep scooped up the glass after a solemn look at Blake's dust-covered clothes and trail-drawn face. He put the second glass before Blake, counted out more money, and tossed it into a can behind the counter. Then he went off, answering an impatient call from a group down the bar. Blake sipped his drink this time, letting it wash the trail dust down his throat. When he had his third drink he turned his back to the counter and glanced around the place. It was a large, high-ceilinged room, but the pall of tobacco smoke screened off the roof lanterns and gave it the cramped look of a cave. Card tables were lined along the far wall, and what space was left around them was filled to overflowing. A section no more than ten feet by twenty had been swept clean and the smell of kerosene came from its boards. Men moving about had to shoulder their way and curses came thick and often from the bulk of the crowd. Despite the swearing, Blake saw that the place was kept orderly and he wondered vaguely who was responsible. It certainly wasn't the little barkeep with the round face and fat, sweating body. Blake's gaze moved on. Saloon girls in feathered and frilled dresses were doing their best to make the customers feel at home. Blake caught the gaze of a slim girl who looked no more than twenty or so. Her immediate interest in him showed in a quick, flashing smile and a slight tilt of her raven-haired head. She kept looking at him until she was caught by the elbow by a cowhand who was unsteady on his feet. Blake saw a frown knit her brow before she was swallowed by the crowd pushing onto the cleared space reserved for dancing. In the background a piano threw out tinny sound which was soon nearly drowned under the stamping of many feet and the swish of skirts. Blake finished his drink and got another from the barkeep who leaned on the counter.

'Dust settlin', stranger?' the little man asked.

Blake nodded. 'On the way.'

'Well, no need to drown yourself, throwin' it down

so quick. Saturdays we stay open late, sometimes till sunup, now and again even after the church bell's rung. Depends on whether the crowd's got religion or not.'

Another call attracted the barkeep's attention and he went away grumbling. Blake shifted to let a couple of cowpokes use his space at the bar, then he saw that he was being stared at by the pretty little redhead again. Her smile was invitingly warm this time, but the scowl from the man at her elbow was anything but companionable. As she was dragged from sight. Blake grinned, then began to thread his way across the room. When he saw the young girl again, she looked away suddenly and ducked out of sight, revealing another woman, a little older, with the sweep of the stairway behind her. She was strikingly attractive but some hard years had caught up with her and brought a light fretwork of lines to her mouth and eyes. She caught and held his look, then she, too, turned away, so he made his way across to the card area where a solid knot of men stood around a center table absorbed in the play. Heeling about on impulse, Blake saw the young redhead and the taller woman still together, no more than ten feet from him.

Once more his look clashed with the tall woman's and he saw her mouth soften a little and a gleam come into her eyes. He heard her say, 'Stick to the hardcase cowboys, Marie, they're more your type.'

The young girl went off, pouting and throwing her head back, and was quickly claimed by a group of cowhands who boisterously welcomed her into their midst. For one brief moment the older woman studied Blake. When she lowered her eyes and turned, he returned his attention to the card game.

Four men sat at the table, heads bowed over large stacks of chips. The bets came fast. Blake's attention went to the youngest of the four, a man no more than twenty-four years old. He had bright red hair, a blotched face and thin hands which shifted nervously. Now he hesitantly eased a stack of chips forward, but then he drew the chips back, cursed, and pushed his cards into the center of the table. His glance at the man on his right was heavy and sullen as the bigger man raked in the pot. The winner was dressed in the manner of gamblers Blake Durant had seen in the bigger towns back east and on the steamers which plied the Mississippi. He had the supremely confident look of a man who was winning and could visualize no end to his affair with Lady Luck.

As hand followed hand and the youth steadily lost, his mood turned sour. He kept counting his diminishing stake, grumbling now and again under his breath. Once he looked directly at Blake and

62

scowled, as if blaming him for his run of bad luck. Blake held his look casually and sipped at his drink.

After a time, one of the other players rose and kicked back his chair noisily. 'Deal me out. I'm in far enough,' he said tightly, and shouldered his way through the crowd, cursing under his breath as he went. The youth wheeled about in his chair and threw a challenging look Blake's way.

'Strikes me the game has you interested, stranger. Like to buy in?'

Blake shook his head, finished his drink and deposited the glass on a wall shelf. He took a pouch from his shirt pocket and started to make himself a cigarette. The youth's lips turned back scornfully. He picked up the pack of cards and shuffled them, his eyes fixed on the remainder of his chips.

He dealt. The betting started and gained momentum.

Blake kept watching the youth, seeing his nervousness increase, his mouth harden. He bought two cards and shuffled his hand before he fingered the cards into a fan, only the very corner of each card showing to his heavy-eyed look. His face remained expressionless but Blake noticed a deepening of the gleam in his hooded eyes. The betting went on until only the young man and the dude-dressed gambler were left.

Sweat gleamed on the young man's upper lip. He packed his cards together and fingered his stake, uncertainty stamped on his face.

'The bet's a hundred, Red,' the dude said. 'Make up your mind.'

The dude sat very still, smoke from a thin cigar drifted past his cool, expressionless eyes. The fingers of his right hand drummed lightly on his face-down cards. The young man stole another look at Blake, then defiance glinted in his blue eyes and he pushed the last of his chips into the center of the table.

'Matched and doubled, Callinan.'

Callinan smiled wryly and went on drumming. He counted the young man's stack, pushed his chips forward to cover the bet, and turned his cards over, 'Three aces.'

The redhead turned over his cards too quickly, his blue eyes bright with excitement. The cards spilled forward untidily and he had to rake them back and fan them for view.

'Four deuces.'

The young man scooped in the pot while Callinan pulled on his lips and tidied his own money before reaching for the cards. The young man looked at Blake Durant again, triumphantly now. Blake gave him a wry smile and walked lazily across the room until he reached the bar again. He was digging up loose change when a woman behind him said, 'Hap, fill the stranger's glass. I'll have one of the same.'

Blake looked into a bright-eyed, rouged face. The woman gave him a guarded smile and looked him over intently.

'You made quite an impression when you walked in, stranger,' she said. 'Three of my girls almost forgot past friendships when they saw you.'

The barkeep brought the drinks and the woman went on, 'Custom of the house to buy a stranger a drink. Come a long way?'

'Some.'

'Figure on staying?' Her eyes went over him again and she made no effort to disguise her approval of what she saw.

'Might.'

'Well, the town can use a couple of new faces. Cowhand, by the look of you.'

Blake shrugged. 'I've eaten my share of herd dust.'

The woman was silent for a time and Blake saw that his lack of cooperation nettled her a little. Finally she said, 'I'm Belle Hudson. I've been running the saloon since my husband passed away two years ago.' Blake saw her stare deepen, as if endeavoring to gauge his reaction to this personal information.

'I'm Blake Durant,' he said.

'Durant.' The woman smiled. 'Suits you, Blake. You've got the name of a man who knows what he wants and mostly gets it. Have I got that correct?'

Blake gave her a vague smile. Then there was a sudden roar from the card tables and he turned to see the young man shouldering his way through the crowd. Several cowhands followed him through, all talking at once, one patting the redhead's back. He caught sight of Blake and Belle and pulled out a handful of money. He slapped it down between them and said exultantly, 'I took Callinan, Belle.'

Blake saw mild surprise on the woman's face. 'Is that so, Red? Well, that's fine, but don't get too carried away. Mr Callinan doesn't stay a loser for long.'

'He's a loser tonight,' Red said. 'Took just one big hand. I called his bluff and cleaned him out to the last dollar.'

Red's friends were grouped behind him, nodding confirmation. The young man studied Blake. 'Have a drink, stranger. Seems you brought me luck.'

Then Red stepped back into his circle of friends and they went out, making a loud racket. Belle Hudson sighed wearily and said, 'One night up, one night down. In the long run, though, Laslo Callinan will get all their money.'

Blake sipped his drink, pushed the change

towards Hap and said, 'The way this town is shaping, I could stay a week and come out in front.'

Belle smiled brightly, standing very close now. Two men came and wished her goodnight. She answered with friendly smiles and then moved even closer to Blake's side.

Looking intently at him, her interest completely frank, she said, 'It gets quieter from now on, which is a blessing. You did say you were staying, Blake, didn't you?'

Blake shrugged. Belle's fresh perfume was very pleasant after the range smells, and her well-formed body was soft against his hard frame. Belle's face told the story of a woman who had known many places, many friendships, and perhaps more than her fair share of disappointments. Her mouth was rather small and the lines on each side suggested she could stop smiling whenever it suited her, which he guessed would be often in a place like this.

The crowd began to thin out. Durant saw Laslo Callinan drinking at the other end of the counter, ignoring the talk of those packed about him. Then Callinan went out on his own, walking quietly. Hap was already cleaning the counter and collecting glasses. The bar-girls, looking slightly disheveled after all the manhandling, were gathered at the bar, having last drinks with men they'd chosen for the night. Their choice of companions struck Blake Durant as a surprising mixture – two cowhands, a tall, well-dressed businessman, a paunchy man in coveralls, a young man who seemed embarrassed over the whole thing, and a thin weed of a man who looked as impatient as a dog on heat.

'. . . so I just kind of stayed on,' Belle was saying. 'There isn't much trouble here. The men get out of hand at times, naturally, but mostly I can persuade them to air their differences outside. When they don't, Sheriff Dowd is never too far away and he takes no nonsense from any of them.'

Blake listened while he watched Hap finish his cleaning chores. Blake was aware of the bar-girls glancing his way now and then, but none of them approached, probably because Belle was making it clear that Blake was her business.

'Where are you staying, Blake?' she asked.

'Haven't bothered to arrange that,' he told her. 'Saw a rooming-house down the street on my way in. Looked suitable.'

'It is,' Belle conceded. 'John Marsden's place. Run good, with a healthy table and no bugs. But for tonight, why don't you stay here? I sometimes have guests stay over – on invitation.'

Blake sipped his drink and gave her no immediate answer. Two of the girls and their escorts went out through the batwings, then the batwings opened again and a man's bulky frame filled them. Blake saw a troubled look spread across Belle's face. He turned and saw Sully Benjamin, backed by a taller man in black. Blake watched the second man sweep the room with a careful look before he edged Benjamin aside and made his way to Hap who was washing glasses in a tub behind the counter. Benjamin hesitated a moment and after rubbing a hand across his drawn features, walked towards the man in black. Belle whispered, 'Wait here, Blake. Don't go yet.'

Blake let her take one step before he pushed out a hand, blocking her way.

'I think it's my business,' he said.

Belle stopped dead in her tracks, lifted her worried gaze from his arm across her bosom to his face. Blake Durant stood warily at her side, his easygoing manner completely gone. In the back of his eyes devils of concentration were asserting themselves. He ignored her look and eased her further back.

Belle remained silent.

Sully Benjamin planted his feet wide, hands swinging at his sides, eyes sparked with bitterness. Then Blake's attention swung to the girls and he saw the red-haired girl in their midst. They were looking anxiously Sully Benjamin's way.

Then Belle said, 'Girls, call it a night. Come on now.' The noise of their hurried exit did not distract Blake's attention from Benjamin and his companion. The back door slammed and the footsteps on the stairway ceased. Belle came into Blake's view, her expression severe.

'What's the trouble, Sully?' she asked. 'You know the rules. The saloon's closed.'

Benjamin jerked a hand at Blake. 'This jasper, Belle, killed Will Pearl.'

Hap tossed his bar rag away and came down the back of the counter quickly. Blake saw Hap's face distort with worry as he ducked under the counter flap and hurried to where Belle stood. Blake shifted a step away from the counter's edge and watched the tall man in black walk towards him. The man's steady, even footsteps rang through the silence. He stopped just short of Blake and smirked as his black eyes ran over Blake's tall body. Then he turned to the right, crossed to the wall near the card tables and leaned against it.

'I'll stand for no trouble in here, Benjamin,' Belle's voice rang out shrilly. 'None from you either, Jud Slater.'

Blake saw a wider, more scornful smile cross the newcomer's face. He ran the name through his head. Jud Slater. He had never heard of him, but Slater's posture, smirking arrogance, and practiced casualness put their stamp on him: gunslinger.

Blake said, coolly, 'I'll handle it, Belle.'

Benjamin scowled at him and spat onto the floor, then his right hand rose and clamped on his gunbelt buckle.

But Belle shifted to where Blake could see her and Hap alongside. Her voice was sharp. 'Benjamin, go on home!'

Blake saw Slater making a cigarette, eyes shining with amusement. Slater's black eyes settled on Blake although he spoke to the saloon woman, 'Belle, Sully's made his call. Nothin' you nor anybody else can do about it. Durant killed his trail friend, so you ain't goin' to stand in the way of Sully, are you?'

'I don't care about that, Slater,' Belle snapped. 'I'll not have my place turned into a—'

'Sully, you're wastin' my time and your own,' Slater cut over her voice. 'Take him if you still mean to.'

Blake saw Benjamin's scowl become uglier. 'I mean to, damn you!'

'Then get on with it.' Blake watched both of them now, Benjamin wetting his lips, Slater eyeing him above cupped hands which shielded a flame. Belle backed away, Hap moving with her. As she went Blake Durant got a quick glimpse of her face, saw her concern for him deepen. He couldn't believe that

71

she felt Benjamin represented a threat to him. So he decided that Slater was the man to worry about. He returned his attention to Benjamin, dismissing Slater for the moment, since the tall gun hand seemed to have drawn out of the argument and had left Benjamin to make the play.

Benjamin braced himself and growled, 'I'm goin' to beat the stuffin' outa you, Durant. Goin' to break you apart.'

He came on, lumbering forward like an over-grown bear, his chest rising under the intake of a deep breath. As Blake waited for Benjamin, his gaze shifted to the stairway and he saw the bar-girls waiting there, their eyes fixed on him.

Then Sully Benjamin swung with a heavy grunt.

Blake side-stepped the first lunge, grabbed Benjamin by the shoulder and wheeled him away. Cursing, Sully Benjamin skidded to a halt. Slater scowled at him from behind a screen of cigarette smoke.

'Take him, damn you!' Slater snapped.

Blake saw Benjamin's shoulders crowd his bull neck. Then the big cowhand turned, his face crimson with anger.

'You're bucking your luck,' Blake told him calmly and stood tall, completely relaxed, hands at his sides. Benjamin gave out another grunt and waded in, mouth wet with saliva, hands swinging wildly. Blake dodged a second time, spun Benjamin about and tripped him up. Sully Benjamin let out a cry and slid across the sawdusted, kerosene-greased floor on his chest and stomach. Slater shifted as Benjamin came his way and slammed a boot onto Sully's head, keeping him from smashing into the wall.

'Seems you're a talker and little else, Sully,' Slater drawled.

Benjamin jolted his head up and swore. He worked from under Slater's boot, shrugged sawdust from his clothes and wiped his hands on his grubby Levis. 'You'll see, Slater, damn you, you'll see!'

Belle called out, 'Benjamin, haven't you made a fool enough of yourself yet? Get on home and let respectable folk get to bed.'

Benjamin was on his feet again, cursing. He glared at Slater, then at Belle and Hap and finally he turned to confront Blake Durant again. Blake blew out a sigh as Benjamin charged again.

This time Benjamin managed to land a punch on the side of Blake's head. Blake gave no indication that the blow hurt but his lips tightened and his shoulders squared as Benjamin launched another attack. Blake's fists cracked into Benjamin's face and stemmed the tide of his advance, then Blake punched him mercilessly with both hands. Benjamin finally reeled back under the punishment and stood away, rubbing a hand across his bleeding face. Then he let out a roar and charged again, all his weight behind a swinging right hand. Blake took the blow on his forearm and then he grasped Benjamin's right wrist and twisted. Benjamin howled, pain distorting his bloated features.

Blake said, 'You're a damn fool, mister.'

Benjamin fell to his knees. Blake pushed him aside and stepped past him. But Benjamin, humiliation seething inside him, whipped back and grabbed at Blake's legs. Blake felt himself going over Benjamin's shoulders. He landed on his feet, spun about, grabbed Sully's hair and dragged him erect. Then Blake hammered his right into Benjamin's face. He felt the big man's nose flatten and another howl came from Sully Benjamin and he crumpled. Blake swung to Jud Slater, as the tall man, face dark, shifted slowly away from the wall.

Slater said, 'Crawl away, Benjamin, you ain't up to this.'

Benjamin, bleeding from the nose and groaning in pain, struggled to his feet. He wiped the blood on his sleeve, took a few staggering steps and growled, 'I ain't crawlin', Slater. I'm goin' to kill him now.'

'Then get on with it.'

Blake moved back to the edge of the counter and

rubbed the knuckles of his right hand on his Levis. He turned Belle's way when he heard her say, 'Hap, get the rifle.' The little barkeep was already on his way through the curtained doorway when Blake said:

'Don't buy in, Belle.'

There was no reply from her but he saw her lips tighten with determination. Sully Benjamin had regained his breath and was circling about, hurt, but riled enough by Slater's disgust to come again. He made a wide movement past Blake before he put his head down and charged. Blake met his lunge with a solid uppercut which sent Benjamin's head jolting back and left him floundering, arms flailing. Blake moved into him, sick of the man's stubbornness. He sank a blow into Benjamin's over-fleshed stomach, doubling him over, then he smashed him back with a right hook which lifted Sully Benjamin inches from the floor before he collapsed in a heap.

Benjamin struggled up again. Hap returned, rifle in hand, and stood close to Belle. She took the gun from him and eased him away.

Hap hesitated, but when Slater straightened, hands curled at his sides, the barkeep called, 'Keep out of it, Slater. Belle don't want no trouble from you.'

Blake had seen the tall man's hand curl. He also noted the viciousness in his black eyes.

Sully Benjamin stood with blood dripping from a gashed eye and a broken nose. His mouth hung slack, swollen. Blake had reduced him to a pitiful hulk. But he felt no sympathy for this bully who would have, given the chance, beaten the Gray boy a second time at the creek.

'Goin' to kill you for this,' Benjamin croaked, and then he went into a crouch, his gun hand dipping. Blake heard Hap call out, 'Belle!' He saw the little man throw himself against the wall. Blake lashed upwards with his boot and caught Benjamin on the wrist. The gun flew high and crashed into the wall. Blake shuffled to him and hammered a fist into his already battered face. Benjamin hit the floor, then crawled along the wall, deep groans coming from him. He reached the back doorway and clung to the chipped jamb.

Slater sent a contemptuous look Benjamin's way and faced Blake Durant. 'You've had your fun,' he said.

Blake sized him up, saw that both his hands were curled above his twin holsters. He saw bleak anger in the man's black eyes and knew he faced a far more dangerous opponent.

Despite his concentration on Slater, Blake's keen ears picked up the scrape of steel on the floor. He turned, saw Sully Benjamin coming up with his gun.

76

Blake Durant's hand moved in a blur of movement, his gun coming out of his holster in one fluid action. The Peacemaker bucked in his fist and a cry came from Belle as Durant's bullet slammed into Benjamin and carried him through the doorway – but not before Benjamin's gun roared and his bullet nicked Blake's ear.

The moment Sully Benjamin disappeared from sight, Blake Durant's interest in him died. He saw shock rise in Belle's face and whipped his body about. Slater's Colts cleared leather and they thundered with Blake's in a room splitting uproar. Blake felt the sharp burn of a bullet past his neck as Slater jerked upright, off balance, and bumped against one of the card tables, the guns falling from his hands. It seemed certain to Blake that Slater would go down, but somehow he stayed erect and clamped his right hand onto a bloodying patch high on his left arm. From his eyes blasted a hate that Blake Durant had seen in few other men.

Belle moved away from the wall and stopped beside Blake. Her look went curiously all over him and finally settled on his expressionless face. Blake watched only Slater, seeing the play of hate in the man's pain-tortured features.

Then Belle said, 'I expect that will settle the matter.'

Beyond Slater's sagged body Blake saw the bar-girls crowded together – but a fierce look from Belle sent them scattering out of sight.

Slater said, 'I'll get you, Durant, sure.'

Blake held his look evenly, the tension slowly going out of him. 'You want to finish it now, mister?' he invited.

Slater, clutching his shoulder, swore under his breath. But defiance showed in his eyes.

'There'll be no more,' Belle said angrily. 'Hap, fetch the sheriff and the doc. Slater, you called a wrong tune – so get on home.'

Jud Slater glared furiously at Belle before shooting a quick look at the doorway through which Sully Benjamin had gone. Then he pushed himself off the buckled table.

'Soon,' he told Blake Durant. 'Real soon.'

With that he picked his guns up from the floor and holstered them. He drew in a ragged breath, turned on his heels, and, walking tall, went out onto the boardwalk. Belle turned and looked intently into Blake Durant's face, her eyes gleaming with deep-seated admiration. Soon Slater's footsteps died and the room was filled with a silence which still had throbs of tension pounding through it.

Belle said, 'I better fix that ear for you, Blake. Come upstairs. I have everything I need there.' Her voice was husky with concern.

Blake fingered his bleeding ear, threw a glance at Benjamin's boots showing in the rear doorway, then without argument let Belle lead the way.

At the top of the stairs, they turned down the passageway and Blake heard a door click closed. Belle moved quickly in front of Blake, opened a door and stepped aside to let him pass. She closed the door quietly behind them and stood there, her gaze warm on him, her bosom heaving. After a quick gasp of breath she hurried into a side room. Blake looked around. The room was neat and everything was carefully arranged, not a thing out of place. The big bed's purple silk cover reminded him of the carpet of wild flowers which sprang up every springtime back home on the plains. From the dresser beside the bed, the strong scent of Belle's perfume came tantalizingly.

Blake settled on the edge of one of the chairs. When Belle came back, he let her wash and tend his wound. That chore finished, she returned the basin and medicines to the other room and loosened the ribbon holding the top of her silken blouse. She gave him a smile and poured a drink from the small wall cabinet against the far wall. The glass she handed him was of fine crystal. Blake eyed her as she touched his neck and caressed his dust-stained skin. Her eyes gleamed warmly with invitation.

'I thought you'd get yourself killed,' she said. 'Sully Benjamin is a stupid fool, but that Jud Slater is another matter. He meant what he said before he left.'

Blake nodded and tossed the drink down. When Belle moved to give him a refill he stood up, saying, 'No thanks, Belle. What I need most is sleep.'

'Stay here, Blake. I told you we have spare rooms . . . for special people.'

'I'm special?'

Belle came to him and slid her hands over his shoulders. She kissed him lightly on the lips, but lingered with her body against his chest, studying him for reaction. 'I think you are, Blake, I really do. It's not just tonight. It was earlier when I first saw you.'

'I've got to see to my horse,' Blake said.

Belle shook her head. 'Hap will do that, Blake. We have stables out back. In the morning, when you're rested, we'll talk. The point is – and I want you to think about it – I can use a good man in my place.'

Blake let himself be led to a small room that was as clean and comfortable as Belle's. He dropped onto the bed and began to pull off his boots. Weariness was swiftly taking hold of him.

'I hope you get to like us, Blake,' Belle said from the doorway. 'Sleep well.'

Blake nodded and watched the door close. He felt

no remorse at shooting Sully Benjamin. And he felt no concern about winging Jud Slater either. They'd asked for it. But it occurred to him that Crimson Falls was a violent place. Will Pearl and Benjamin were dead, and Slater was going home with a wound.

In addition there was Belle Hudson, a woman making no bones about her interest in him. He liked the woman, saw a lot of good in her. At most other times, he might have felt obliged to take care of her needs. But there was always that memory of the past, of another woman, of feelings that would never leave him.

Blake closed his eyes, blanked his mind and willed his body to relax. And finally sleep came . . .

SIX

THE LAW AND
BLAKE DURANT

Blake Durant slept the sleep of the weary. When sunlight filtered through the window drapes onto his tanned face, he stirred, momentarily unsure of where he was. In the corner of the room was a basin of clean water with a towel hanging over the rail beneath it. There was a cake of fresh-scented soap near the basin, beside his own razor. Durant lay completely still for some time, letting his mind swing back to the disturbing events of the previous night. He lifted his hands and ran them through his hair. The pain which had been in his head the previous evening had gone.

Durant swung to the floor. His clothes had been brushed down and folded neatly. Quickly he washed, shaved and dressed. He was ready to leave the room when there was a faint knocking. Durant opened the door and looked into the face of the young redhead who had shown so much interest in him the night before.

'You're up,' she said. Then Durant watched the color rise in her face as she added, 'Belle said to see that you got anything you wanted. There's coffee downstairs in the kitchen or whisky if you prefer.'

'Coffee will do fine.'

'Then go straight down the stairs. Hap will show you the way from there and I'll fix the room for you.'

She slipped into the room past him and started to strip the bed. 'I saw you kill that Sully Benjamin last night,' she said. 'He had it coming, always looking for trouble and abusing people.'

Durant wiped a finger across his brow and took hold of the door, but the young woman, plainly keen on talking now that she had him alone, asked:

'Will you be staying, maybe working for Belle, Mr Durant?'

As Durant held her look he realized that he had not made up his mind about his future movements. 'We'll see,' he said.

She brightened. 'If you do, I think it will be fine. I'm Marie. I'm to see you get looked after, no matter what you want.'

She was standing perfectly erect now, her blouse pulled tight across her firm bosom. Her face was too rouged but the youth shone from her eyes. Her lips were red, moist, and she turned a pink tongue across them.

'That's fine, Marie,' said Durant and went out.

Marie listened to his firm footsteps along the corridor, her head tilted and a smile of satisfaction playing along the corners of her well-formed mouth. After a minute she began to hum to herself.

Durant went downstairs to find Hap already working behind the counter, getting things ready for the day's expected busy trade. He gave Durant a curt nod, saying:

'Guess Marie's already told you, eh? Benjamin didn't make it.'

'She mentioned it.'

'I fetched the undertaker, Patterson, and he took his body away. I guess Tom Dowd will want to see you soon. Just arrived back from checking out some trouble near Gopher's Hollow.'

Durant asked for directions to the kitchen and Hap showed him the way. Belle was waiting for him. She gave him a warm look and poured coffee for him, then went suddenly quiet, gaze lowered, face flushed a little. Durant left her to her thoughts. The coffee was hot and strong. There was nobody else in the kitchen so they sat, making small talk. Then, his coffee finished, Blake rose, excused himself and crossed the room to the yard. Sundown was frisking with a glossy-coated piebald filly and paid him no more heed than a nicker of recognition. Durant leaned over the rail and watched the play of the two horses. He turned when footsteps sounded behind him and looked into the flat, expressionless face of a big man with a tin star on his chest.

'Durant?' the man said.

Blake Durant nodded.

The lawman was silent for a few moments, then he said, 'I'm Tom Dowd. I've already talked to Belle and Hap about last night. Seems Benjamin asked for all he got.'

Durant liked the look of the lawman. Dowd had a way of talking straight into a man's face with no uncertainty showing. His hands were steady and he had deep-set eyes and a solid chin.

'Which ties up Sully Benjamin pretty well,' Dowd said. 'The rest might not be so easy.'

'What rest?' Durant asked.

'Slater and Cowley.'

'Slater knows where he stands with me,' Durant said.

'I heard there was a threat made, Durant. I don't like things hanging in the air, not in my town. Slater has never been the kind to let a slug in his arm stop him. When he gets well again, he won't forget you.'

'That's his business,' Durant clipped. 'He can make of it what he likes.'

Dowd's lips thinned. He pushed himself off the rail and smoothed his hands down the side of his Levis. His big gun looked lethal in its oiled holster.

'It's my business, too, Durant. Nobody's holding anything against you on account of last night. Belle's not one to tell lies or make up excuses for any man. You impressed her plenty and she's damn hard to impress where strangers and drifters are concerned.'

Blake straightened, working the cramp out of his shoulders. He felt completely rested yet restlessness gnawed at him.

Dowd said flatly now, 'Okay, I'll put it plain. You killed Will Pearl, so I'm told, and now Sully Benjamin. To top that you put a slug in Jud Slater's arm. So your tally is three of Gus Cowley's men out of business and Cowley ain't the kind of man to think kindly of anybody who does that to his outfit. Cowley's set for his end-of-the-year round-up and he gets so keen to have things run smoothly for him that he stops his men coming to town for weekend drinks even. He ain't goin' to like it one bit, having you in town, after what you've done.'

Durant wasn't in the least worried. He said, 'Sheriff, we've got nothing to talk about. I mind my own business and expect the same of other people. Now I'll have a drink, pay my respects to Belle and then figure out what comes next – all on my own.'

Dowd licked his lips and stood back. 'You're gonna stay in town and wait for trouble to come?'

'I didn't say that.'

'What the hell did you say then, mister? Hell, can't you see the predicament I'm in? I've got law and order to uphold and I'm damned if I can see that being done with Slater and Cowley hollerin' for your hide. Let's get one thing straight, Durant. I don't give a damn what kind of hellion drifts into town. If he puts me out, then he answers to me for it.'

'That's natural,' Durant said as he moved into the kitchen. Belle looked up sharply and watched Dowd stride angrily away. She smiled hesitantly at Blake while rising to her feet and smoothing her skirt over slim hips.

'Everything all right?' she asked.

'Sure, fine.'

Her look brightened. 'I'm glad. Tom Dowd is a fine man and good for the town. But he gets a little headstrong when things don't go quite his way. What have you decided to do?'

'I haven't, Belle. I'm obliged for the room and coffee.'

'You're welcome, Blake, any time. By the way, I thought a great deal about you last night, in fact I couldn't get to sleep for a long time thinking about you.'

'I'm mighty flattered,' Durant said, but there was no promise in his voice.

'Well, anyway, I expect you'll look the town over a little and judge for yourself whether you'll stay or not,' Belle said. 'If you do stay, have lunch with me at noon. I promise not to pester you with another offer of a job. But it would be good having you about until you find what you really want.'

Durant gave her a smile, a brief wave, and went out. He crossed to the bar and ordered a whisky from Hap, then he looked casually about the room, finding it much different than it had been last night, roomier certainly and a great deal quieter. Hap worked diligently for some time before he took up a position directly opposite Durant. Two early customers came in, one already drunk, the other standing so stiffly he seemed afraid to breathe. Hap served them, shaking his head in sympathy for both, then he asked Durant:

'How come you run into the Cowley boys in the first place, Mr Durant? On the way through?'

Durant nodded noncommittally.

Hap, showing no annoyance, went right on, 'Hard bunch, near every one of them, but not as bad as them what used to come through here in the old days and tear the town apart. That was when the railroad was just finished. Murderous gangs rode through and they kilt faster than graves could be dug. We used to have a kind of hell here in town of a Saturday night. But then things simmered down like they always do when law and order comes. That was when men like Cowley came and sunk taproots and showed they meant to stay and didn't want no nonsense. Cowley did a lot for the town in those days and I guess lots of folk kinda close their eyes when some of his bunch go hellin' it up now and again.'

Durant finished his drink and asked for another which Hap promptly fetched for him. The barkeep talked on as if nobody had interrupted him. 'Town needed men like Cowley in them days, but I don't reckon they need them as much now. Cowley's maybe too fixed in his ways and can't change and maybe that just ain't no good, for anybody.'

Hap's look backed up his talk; solid, steady, full of meaning. Durant watched him closely but when he made no reply to the barkeep, Hap went on his way, serving more customers who had just come in. One of them, the red-haired card player, gave Durant a quick nod and looked eagerly towards the vacant card tables. A hint of disappointment showed in his blue eyes but quickly went as friends crowded about him, talking a treat about the last night's game and the red-haired young man's success.

After his second drink, Durant left the saloon and moved easily along the warped boardwalk. A slight breeze whipped up dust in the street. Already a lot of people were moving about; some of them cast guarded looks at Durant. He walked to the extreme end of town and looked into the foothills. Out there a widow would be stirring and a boy setting about his ranch chores. Durant realized with a faint smile that his thoughts had turned a great deal to the Gray woman and her troubles.

He was still there, idling away the time, when two riders burst around the corner of the street and went on fast, their horses kicking up heavy dust. Durant recognized Arch Briller but he took more interest in the other rider, a raw-boned, surly featured man with a no-nonsense look about him. Durant made his way back down the street, guessing that this was Gus Cowley about whom he had heard so much and little of it good. But Cowley looked no meaner or more aggressive than the usual run of ranchers Blake Durant had known at home or had met during his drifting. The hard life, the continual battle against the elements, the never-ending annoyance of rustlers, trouble-makers and the like, brought to most of those ranchers' faces hard lines of determination and stubbornness.

Blake reached Center Street and saw the two of them on the boardwalk. Cowley glared at the law office, then he shouldered Briller out of his way and snapped:

'I'm goin' to the bank. Stay out of trouble.'

Blake watched Briller hitch up both horses as Cowley walked across the street. Briller then gave the batwing doors of the saloon a long look before he wiped his mouth on the back of his hand. He approached the saloon cautiously, took a furtive look inside and, evidently finding it to his liking, went in.

Durant drew up outside the saloon, saw Cowley enter the front door of the bank opposite and for the devilment of it, pushed the batwing doors open. Arch Briller already had beer froth on his fat lips. He was turned halfway to watch the street doorway and when he saw Durant enter, his glass dropped to the counter and shattered.

Briller stood there as if nailed to the floor, his face white, his breath locked inside him. Durant went to Briller, conscious that Belle was watching him from the end passageway and that Hap, in his usual careful way, had given her a signal. Briller went to step past

Blake. But Blake's hand swung out, fastened on his shirt and pulled him back.

'No need to hurry off,' Blake said.

Briller spluttered something under his breath, wiped his mouth twice and, giving the red-headed man and his now-curious group a nervous glance, said nervously, 'You . . . you got no cause to crowd me, Durant. I ain't harmed you none.'

'That's the truth,' Durant said, then he beckoned to Hap and ordered two drinks. Briller shook his head at Hap, but the barkeep brought a rye and a beer and placed them before Durant.

Durant pushed the beer towards Briller and said, 'Looks like you had a hard ride, mister. Drink?'

Briller looked uncertainly at the glass, nodded grimly and then muttered, 'Well, don't mind if I do, Durant. Hell, no sense in us cutting at each other.'

'No sense at all, Briller,' was the cool reply. Hap moved off, giving Belle a thoughtful look. Belle shrugged then headed for the stockroom. Blake drank slowly, swilling the rye in his mouth and looking for all the world like a cowhand settled in for a day's casual drinking. But Briller remained stiff beside him and plainly eager to be gone.

Briller made short work of his beer. Then, nodding to Durant he said, 'Well, I got to be going. Mr Cowley's waiting for me.'

'Cowley come to town often?' Durant asked. 'Or is today special?'

Briller stole a look down the counter as Laslo Callinan came in. The gambler was dressed nattily in a town suit and had a cigar protruding from his thin-lipped mouth. He gave Durant a look, then a nod, and crossed to the card tables where he proceeded to tear the seal off a fresh pack of cards. The red-haired young man straightened at the counter, grinned at his friends and walked to the table where he pulled out a chair and took a roll of money from his pocket. Durant saw Callinan lift his eyebrows into an arch of feigned surprise, then push the cards towards Red for cutting. The redhead's friends quickly caught up their beers and left the counter empty for Briller and Blake Durant, who turned now and looked calmly at Briller.

'Seems you're worried about something,' Durant said quietly.

'No, no, Durant . . . I'm fine.'

'Maybe you feel the loss of Benjamin.'

Briller gulped uneasily and shook his head. 'Nope, Sully weren't no great friend of mine.' Suddenly he straightened, a faint flicker of courage showing in his eyes. 'Look here, Durant, what do you want with me? I ain't ever done you no harm. I didn't even hit the Gray kid and I didn't come to town after you like

Benjamin and Slater. For mine, I don't want nothin'
to do with you, ever.'

'Why come to town today?' Durant asked.

'Mr Cowley came to see the banker about the Gray
mortgage. He—' Briller's mouth clamped shut.

'Go on,' Blake said.

Briller shook his head. 'It ain't none of your business, Durant. Hell, leave me alone, will ya? Cowley's
mad enough at what's happened now.'

'Does he intend to push her and the boy off their
property?' Durant asked.

Briller swallowed. 'Well, hell, Mr Cowley's got the
option on that place and it's a damn nuisance havin'
their fences stoppin' his way across.'

Blake Durant swirled the rye in his glass and gazed
into its depth. Then he saw Briller stiffen and
without looking he knew who had come in. His eyes
lifted to Gus Cowley.

Cowley stood just inside the batwings. His stare
settled on Durant and quick respect rose in his eyes
though his mouth twisted down sullenly at the
corners. He came forward with firm, deliberate steps.

'Durant?'

'Yep, Cowley.'

Cowley studied Durant for a long time before he
waved Briller to get drinks. When the hired hand
eagerly moved along the bar to Hap, Cowley said:

'Well, it seems you've set yourself to make trouble for me, Durant. Killing two of my men, wounding another. How long do you think I'll let that go on?'

Durant shrugged. 'You tell me, Cowley.'

Gus Cowley read the insolence in Blake's tone. His face tightened and his hooked nose curled a little more as his mouth pinched tight.

'I'll tell you how much longer,' Cowley said. 'Not a minute. Even now I should smash you down like the cur you are.'

A hard shine entered Blake's eyes. 'Your men stole a boy's calves, Cowley. Is that how loose a rein you have on them?'

'No damn fault of mine, Durant. I gave strict orders for the widow and her boy to be left alone. But I didn't bargain for a drifter like you buying into my affairs, and I don't mean for it to happen again. Take due warning, Durant. Get out of my territory if you know what's good for you.'

Cowley glared at Briller and snapped, 'Damn you, Briller, bring the drinks down.'

Briller came quickly, handing Cowley a beer which the big man pushed back along the counter. Cowley turned to Hap.

'You! Get me a man's drink. Double!'

Hap poured the drink as Blake Durant looked calmly at Cowley. Hap brought the drink to Cowley

who tossed it down and looked fiercely at Durant.
Suddenly Cowley grabbed Briller and pushed him
towards the batwing doors. Then he turned to Blake
and grimaced. 'Remember what I tell you now,
Durant. Get out of this town, get out of my territory.
If you don't it'll be more than Jud Slater who'll come
after you.'

Durant let him go. He heard Cowley's heavy footsteps outside and saw Hap frowning at him. He
smiled to himself and finished his drink. As he left
the saloon he saw Belle. Her face held a puzzled
look. He went into the street and stood there a
moment, watching Gus Cowley and Arch Briller stepping into their saddles. Cowley's brutish look swung
onto him again but without another word the
rancher kicked his horse into a run.

Blake Durant scratched a hand behind his neck
and leaned against an overhang post watching the
dust settle. He made himself a cigarette, ignoring
Sheriff Dowd when the lawman passed him. As he
smoked the cigarette, Blake's face was thoughtful.

Jessica Gray stood in the doorway and watched the
sleeping form of her son. A smile touched at her soft
mouth. He was trying so hard to be a man ... the
man he thought his father had been. But no one
knew better than Jessica that her husband had not

been a strong man. A 'loser', Gus Cowley had called him. Maybe. But she had loved him and had stood by him every inch of the way.

Blake Durant. There was a man. Jessica walked to the front door, opened it, looked out at the night. After a moment she went onto the porch. It was a beautiful night. The sky was full of stars. She looked for the Big Dipper, the Little Bear, the Small Dipper, found them all. Then a star fell, tracing a line halfway across the sky. When you saw a falling star and made a silent wish, then God was listening, and if your wish was unselfish enough, it would be granted.

Jessica closed her eyes. What should she wish for? Her thoughts turned to Blake Durant and she folded her arms over her breasts and squeezed. She could feel her breasts swell with desire and suddenly she was hungry for the touch of his hands. She opened her blouse and placed a hand against her throat. The hand moved down and in her imagination it was his hand . . . gentle but insistent . . . his hand, pressing against her flesh, arousing passion from her depths, making her hips sway, setting up a pulsing in her loins and arousing a hunger in her that could be satisfied only by—

No!

She lifted her hand away and grasped the porch railing, breathing heavily, her head bowed. After a while she went down the porch steps and walked beyond the clump of cottonwoods. There was the cross that marked her husband's grave. She stopped short of the grave and a wave of shame moved through her. Then she took a deep breath. She had loved Tom, had been a good wife to him. There was no reason for feeling shame. She couldn't help being a woman, having a woman's desires . . .

She walked to the side of the grave. The flowers she'd planted near the cross were wilted. She watered them every day, but the searing sun was too much for the fragile blooms. Rain was needed. There was something in rain that brought life with it.

She looked at the cross. 'I'm sorry, Tom,' she murmured. 'It isn't that I don't love you or that I . . .' But she couldn't find words to explain how she felt. She stood there by the grave for a long time, and finally a kind of peace came. It was as though he understood and was telling her.

She didn't go straight back to the house. She walked to the vegetable garden behind it. The spinach leaves were small and wrinkled. The tops of the carrots were dry, dead looking. Cabbage and cauliflower had refused to grow at all. She kicked at a clod of earth and even in the darkness she could see the small plume of dust. Dust and death. Had there ever been anything else? This was mean, heartless country. But back in Boston was a big house, wealth . . .

'We have rooms we never use,' her mother had said in her last letter. 'Please, darling, come home and bring Jesse to us. He'll receive a good education here, and neither of you will ever want for anything . . .'

Home.

Where was home? She had thought it was here. It could have been here. But not now. She had nothing left to fight with. Tomorrow the mortgage fell due. If Mr Darrett at the bank didn't grant an extension . . .

She shook her head so hard that the back of her neck hurt, but she couldn't clear her mind of the whirling thoughts that wouldn't let sleep come. She walked. To the empty corral, to the grassless pasture-land beyond. She walked until weariness came, then she returned to the house and fell onto her bed.

I'll be right out,' Jessica answered. She dried the last of the breakfast dishes, removed her apron, then went into the bedroom where she brushed her long auburn hair. After that she looked at herself in the mirror. Shadows beneath her eyes told of the few hours of sleep she'd had. Her lips looked bloodless. Perhaps a touch of powder and some rouge . . .

Moments later she looked at herself again criti-cally. Better. But the gingham dress, though clean and freshly ironed, showed all the signs of long wear. In Boston she'd have a wardrobe closet full of dresses and shoes and frilly under things . . .

She turned away from the face that looked at her from the mirror. Her gaze moved over the room. Bare boards, a makeshift dressing table, an old bed. She walked into the kitchen. A table, three chairs, a cupboard Tom had made from old barn boards. It was a poor little house, yet tears welled in her eyes at the thought of leaving it.

'Come on, Ma, hurry up, willya?' Jesse called.

'Coming.'

Jessica walked onto the porch and down the steps. Jesse sat on the hard buckboard seat. He tied up the reins as Jessica walked around the rig, then he leaned down to help her up.

'Thank you, son.'

'Nice day, Ma, ain't it? Looks like maybe we'll get some rain later on.'

'Looks like we might,' she said, holding back a smile. Just about every morning Jesse foresaw rain.

'We'll get into town right when the bank opens,' Jesse informed her. 'That's good, Ma. It means Mr Darrett won't have any people in his office. He's a nice man, Mr Darrett.'

'A fine man, son.'

Jesse hit out with the reins and clucked his tongue

and the old mare went into a half-hearted canter.

'Don't push old Nellie too hard,' Jessica cautioned.

'Won't have to, Ma. That's why I wanted this early start. We can give Nellie a rest and a drink at Carter Creek; that's just about the halfway mark to town.'

'You think of everything, don't you, Jesse?'

The boy drew himself up importantly. 'It's a man's job, Ma. A man's gotta do the thinkin' for a woman.'

'That's certainly so, son.'

The rig bounced along, the rusted springs under the seat protesting loudly with each bump.

'One of these days I'll get you a new rig,' Jesse said after a while. 'And then I'll go to the horse sales at the county seat and I'll buy you the prettiest Tennessee walkin' horse you ever saw.'

'That'll be real fine, Jesse.'

He looked up at the brassy sky. 'All we need is a little rain. When we get some rain everything'll be better, you'll see.'

It would take a lot more than rain to solve their problems, she thought, but she said nothing to Jesse. He was only a boy, and a boy needed his hopes and his dreams . . .

Old Nellie was in a frisky mood that morning and she got them to Carter Creek with time to spare. Jesse unhitched the mare and led her to the water.

'Water's nice and cool,' Jesse said. 'Why don't you put your feet in the water, Ma? Make you feel good?'

'That's a fine idea,' Jessica said. She climbed down from the seat and walked to the grassy bank where she removed her shoes. Then she sat on the bank and dangled her feet in the water.

'How's that, Ma?'

'It's a luxury, son.'

Jessica closed her eyes. The water did feel good. She listened to the gentle run of the creek, the calling of birds, and then her thoughts turned again to the tall, tight-lipped man who rode the black stallion. 'Blake Durant . . .' She opened her eyes, surprised at the sound of her own voice. She looked towards Jesse, who still stood in the creek with the mare. He hadn't heard her.

Would she see Blake Durant in town, she wondered? He probably spent his spare time in saloons – but surely not this early in the day. Perhaps he'd be walking around, or maybe he'd be on the hotel verandah talking to some of the locals. But he was a handsome man, a virile man. There were saloon girls in town and some of them were pretty. She drew in her breath as there was suddenly an odd pain in her stomach. She was jealous! The realization puzzled her.

There were splashing sounds as Jesse walked the

mare from the creek. He looked over at her and said, 'Stay there a while, Ma. Plenty of time. I spotted an apple tree across the creek. After I harness Nellie I'll go over and see if I can pick some red ones.'

'That'll be nice, Jesse.'

She reached down and swirled her hand in the water. A frightened minnow darted away. When the ripples were gone she saw her reflection. Did Blake Durant think she was pretty? She remembered the strange way he had looked at her, as though she reminded him of someone. Of course, there had to be women in his past – maybe there was one special woman.

She slapped at the water, annoyed with herself. Here she was thinking about a man who was plainly a drifter. Why for all she knew he might be twenty miles or more away, heading for another town. But Durant had gone out of his way to help her and Jesse, and she'd always be grateful to him for that. Still, he wasn't the kind of man who'd settle down with a woman so she was wasting her time even thinking about him. Besides, it was selfish of her to hope that Durant might be in town. It would be dangerous for him to stay there. He'd killed one of Cowley's men and he'd humiliated two of them. Cowley wouldn't be likely to forget such an incident. He might even send that terrible man Slater after Durant. She shivered at the thought. Slater was a heartless killer. Bloodlust was written in his eyes.

'Hey, how about this?' Jesse called from across the creek. In each hand he held two large, red apples.

She said, 'You're nothing short of a marvel, Jesse, that's what you are.'

Jesse wore a broad grin as he waded across the shallow creek.

Griff Darrett stood up behind his desk as Jessica Gray entered his office. He was a tall, paunchy man with a florid face and an easy smile. In his black town suit and white shirt he presented an imposing figure. A diamond pin glittered in his cravat.

'Please be seated, Mrs Gray,' he said in a rich baritone as he indicated the leather-upholstered chair beside his desk.

Jessica thanked him with a smile and sat down. Darrett waited until she was comfortably seated before he lowered his long frame into his swivel chair.

'I – I'm here about the mortgage,' Jessica said hesitantly.

'Yes.' The smile left his lips and he shuffled among the papers on his desk. 'I was just looking at the note your late husband signed.'

'The note is due today,' she said.

'Yes, my dear, I'm aware of that. And so is Mr Cowley. I had a talk with him only yesterday.'

Jessica nodded. 'He wants my place.'

'Wants it badly,' Darrett said.

'But you're holding the note,' she said.

'I must correct you, Mrs Gray. The bank is holding the note.'

'Isn't that the same thing?'

'I'm afraid not. I run the bank but I don't own it – not completely, at any rate. You see, Mrs Gray, I too signed a note. Several months ago, the bank's biggest depositor, Mr Cowley, decided to withdraw his money. This came as a complete surprise to me. I – I was unable to give him the money. It wasn't because I'd done anything dishonest – I'd lent out too much money on mortgages. The only way I could give Mr Cowley his money was to foreclose and then sell various properties. I couldn't very well do that, so I borrowed a great deal of money from Mr Cowley. In consideration, I had to meet one condition . . . I am not permitted to give extensions on mortgages. I'm sorry, terribly sorry, Mrs Gray.'

Jessica looked down at her hands, defeat written in her face. She said, 'Mr Cowley did that only so he could get my place.'

Darrett nodded in agreement but didn't speak.

'What happens now?' Jessica asked.

'Well, the bank will have to foreclose tomorrow morning, at which time Mr Cowley has only to meet the payment of your late husband's note, plus interest, of course. The property will then be his. However, Mr Cowley has no wish to leave you destitute, Mrs Gray. He told me that he's willing to give you two hundred dollars. I understand you have people in Boston?'

'Yes. My parents.'

'The two hundred dollars will more than pay for your journey. Then there will be incidentals, of course – clothing and so on.' Darrett sighed and got to his feet. 'I – I just want you to know, Mrs Gray, that I would gladly let you have an extension if the choice were mine.'

Jessica smiled at him. 'I know you would, Mr Darrett, and I understand your position.'

There was warmth in his smile. 'Thank you. This – this has been one of the worst mornings of my life Your kindness and understanding have made it much easier for me.' He looked around as though afraid someone might be listening. 'There is one way out. Do you know anyone who will advance you the money to pay the note?'

She shook her head.

'I would let you have it from my personal funds,' he said, 'but Mr Cowley would insist on knowing where the money came from.'

'I don't want you to get into trouble because of me,' Jessica said, rising. 'I know that Mr Cowley is a hard, vindictive man.'

'A completely ruthless man, Mrs Gray. When he sets his mind on something, he doesn't let anything or anyone get in his way. He's determined to own this entire valley. Once he has your property he'll be able to control the water supply. Then everyone will be under the Cowley thumb – and that includes me.'

Jessica offered her hand and Darrett took it. She said, 'Perhaps I should feel sorry for you and the others who'll have to—' She turned away abruptly.

'Is something wrong?' Darrett asked, then he saw her shoulders shake and it was obvious she was sobbing. He looked around helplessly. 'I wish there was something I could do ...'

'It's all right,' she said, getting control of herself. 'A woman's weakness, Mr Darrett.'

'I'm not looking at a weak woman,' he said feelingly.

Keeping her back to him, she dabbed at her eyes with a handkerchief, then she forced a smile as she turned to face him.

'Goodbye, Mr Darrett, and thank you for all your efforts on my behalf. When will Mr Cowley want us to leave?'

'Tomorrow, I'm afraid. But if you need some help in packing . . .'

'My son and I will manage.'

'I'll see that you have seats on tomorrow's train east. Just come here to the bank in your buckboard and I'll give you the balance of Mr Cowley's two hundred dollars. If you get here in the morning you'll have time to shop; the train doesn't leave until three in the afternoon.'

'Thank you, Mr Darrett.' She started towards the door, then stopped as a sudden thought struck her. 'There's the buckboard and Nellie, the mare. They're not part of the property listed in the mortgage.'

'I'll be glad to buy the rig and the horse,' Darrett said.

'No. I just want to be sure that Nellie will have a good home. She's served us faithfully and well.'

'I'll keep her with my horses,' Darrett said. 'She'll get the best of care, I assure you. If there's any other way I can help you, don't hesitate to tell me.'

'There's nothing else.'

'Perhaps you'll think of something.'

Jessica opened the office door. As she closed it behind her, she heard Darrett say in a low voice:

'I am sorry . . .'

Jesse was seated on the buckboard, waiting. There

was excitement in his glittering eyes.

'Ma, I just saw Mr Durant go into the saloon. Maybe I could go in there and invite him out to supper tonight or—' He stopped as he saw the expression on his mother's face. 'Mr Darrett gave us the extension, didn't he?'

She lowered her gaze and shook her head.

'But – but he's gotta give us the extension, Ma!'

'He can't.'

Jesse got to his feet, rage twisting at his young face. 'He's a liar if he says he can't! This is his bank – he's got plenty of money!'

'Jesse, there's nothing we can do . . .'

'But there's somethin' Mr Durant can do! Ma, I'm gonna go and have a talk with him.'

SEVEN

NO STREET FOR WOMENFOLK

Belle descended the stairs as Durant returned to the saloon. Ignoring everybody else in the bar-room, she crossed to his side. Hap brought her a drink which she allowed Durant to pay for. She was silent for a while, then she turned to face him and said:

'I know you're not a man who backs down to anybody. Last night you proved it to me. But why did you let Gus Cowley call you down like that in front of all those people?'

'He said nothing that mattered,' Blake told her. Although his reply made her frown at first, gradually her expression lightened.

Before they could continue the conversation, Tom Dowd entered the saloon. He checked the card tables and saw Red playing poker with Callinan. The redhead sat hunched, eyes downcast, no loud boasting coming from him this time. His friends had thinned down to a pair and they looked worried.

Dowd walked to the bar, touched his hat to Belle and looked at Blake.

'Hear you ran into Cowley.'

'Yep.'

'And side-stepped him.'

Durant shrugged. Dowd settled down over his drink, swirling it around. 'Sensible thing to do. Saves us both a lot of trouble. I guess that now, havin' settled that business to the satisfaction of both parties, you'll be moving on.'

'It depends,' Blake said, with a look at Belle. Her face colored and she smiled shyly back at him. Blake noticed that Dowd didn't miss this by-play between them as the lawman downed his drink. Dowd wiped his mouth, set down the shot glass and gave another touch of his hat to Belle. Then he glanced at Blake.

'Maybe this is goodbye. I sure hope so.'

Blake said nothing. Dowd turned and left the saloon. He wasn't gone more than a minute when there was a scraping of a chair at the card table and

Red's booming voice:

'It ain't natural, Callinan! You won every damn hand in the last hour!'

'Luck of the game, boy,' the gambler said softly.

'Don't call me boy!'

'No disrespect meant.'

Silence settled again. Blake watched Red count his chips and grab for the cards Callinan dealt.

'He'll learn – too late,' Belle said dryly.

'Learning comes hard to some,' Blake said. Then he turned at the sound of the batwings being slammed open. A look of surprise crossed his features as he saw Jesse Gray take a few steps into the saloon and stop, his gaze taking Blake in, then shifting to Belle.

'I think this young feller wants to talk to me,' Blake said.

'Got to fix my hair anyhow,' Belle said. Then she lowered her voice. 'Blake, I know that's the Gray boy. I also know how bad Cowley wants the Gray property. You watch yourself.'

'I'll do that,' Blake said with a smile. 'Now you go fix that beautiful hair.'

She smiled back. 'Nicest thing you've said to me.' And she walked off and went up the stairs.

Jesse remained near the bat wings. Blake grinned at him, waved him to the bar. The boy came forward, slowly at first, then in a stumbling rush.

'I think Hap can get you a sarsaparilla,' Blake said.

Jesse shook his head. 'I – I came into town with ma,' he said hesitantly.

Blake grasped the boy's shoulder. 'You got trouble, partner?'

Jesse nodded.

'Well, how about you tell me what it is.'

'It's money trouble, Mr Durant.'

Blake smiled. 'It usually is.'

Jesse looked down at his boots. 'Seems like I'm always comin' to you.'

Blake's grip tightened on the youngster's shoulder. 'Maybe that's just how I want it. Now, look. You tell me why your ma's in town and why you look like the world suddenly dropped right out from under you.'

'We got no money at all,' Jesse said, the words coming in a rush. 'Ma can't meet the mortgage note pa took out on the place. We figgered the weather'd break and things'd be better for us – grass for the cattle, vegetables for ma and me. But now we – we— '

Jesse's voice broke. Blake rolled a cigarette and waited for the boy to get control of himself. Finally Jesse said:

'Ma had a talk with Mr Darrett at the bank. We

gotta get off the property – then that skunk Cowley's gonna take over, just like he always wanted to.'

Blake shook his head. 'Gus Cowley isn't going to take over, son.'

'But we can't pay that note!'

Blake grasped the boy's arm. 'Now you listen to me. You tell your ma to have Mr Darrett with her. I'll be outside to see both of them in five minutes. You got that, Jesse?'

'Yeah, but—'

'You just do like I say. Pronto.'

Blake turned his back to the boy and Jesse shuffled off frowning.

Blake sighed. Something deep inside him had been stirred by the boy's mother. His sympathy for her was something he just could not ignore.

Blake let out a tired smile. Nothing seemed to go right for him in Crimson Falls. Then Belle joined him, fresh and smiling. 'Just ran a brush through it,' she said.

Blake cooled her enthusiasm by saying, 'I'm cutting out for a time, Belle.'

Her face showed disappointment. Blake turned away from her and saw Jesse's face pressed against the glass of the saloon window. He finished his drink and slid the glass along the clean counter.

'The Grays?' Belle asked.

'They've had it rough,' Blake replied.

Belle gave a twisted smile. 'Mrs Gray?'

Blake's face carried no expression and he said nothing. Belle grabbed his wrist and dug her nails in hard.

'I'm sorry I said that, Blake. Terribly sorry. It was wrong of me.'

Blake smiled wryly. 'Nobody's sore at you, Belle. Only obliged.'

He went into the yard and saddled Sundown. The big black had his eye on a glossy-coated brown filly at the far end of the yard. The filly was shifting about excitedly, plainly baiting Sundown. But Sundown submitted to the saddling and when Blake hit the leather, he went straight for the gate. Only when he was through it did he swing back and nicker. Then he made a playful lunge, moved into a brisk canter and, black mane gleaming, went up the saloon alleyway.

On the main street, Mrs Gray and Jesse sat in an old buckboard outside the bank. Darrett stood beside the buckboard. Blake rode up to them, aware that Belle was watching from the saloon batwings. The young widow's face was pale and strained and her lips were pressed tightly together. Further along the street, Sheriff Tom Dowd leaned against an over-hang post trying to look inconspicuous as he dragged on a cigarette. And, on the high verandah above Belle Hudson, Marie brushed her gleaming red hair, making no effort to disguise her interest in the proceedings below.

Blake guided Sundown behind the buckboard and nodded to the banker, Griff Darrett. Then he said, 'I'm meeting Mrs Gray's note.'

Jessica Gray gasped.

'We'll settle right now,' Blake said. 'That all right with you, Mr Darrett?'

The banker nodded, smiled. 'That'll be just fine, Mr Durant.'

'But – but why?' Jessica Gray asked.

Blake turned to her. 'It's a good investment, Mrs Gray.'

She stared into his gaze and her eyes moistened. 'I – Mr Durant, I don't know what to—'

'Say nothing,' he clipped out. 'It's a business proposition.'

'But we won't be able to repay you for a long time. Perhaps we'll never be able to, what with the drought and—'

'Droughts lift,' Blake said. 'Don't you worry. We'll work it out. You see, I intend to look after my investment, and the only way to do that is to be right there.'

'You're gonna work for us?' Jesse asked excitedly.

'With us,' Jessica Gray corrected. 'Mr Durant is a

116

partner now, Jesse.'

The boy's face lit up. 'That's great, Ma!' He turned to Blake. 'Gee, Mr Durant, maybe you can teach me how to shoot and—'

'Hush,' his mother admonished. She looked at Blake, gratitude plainly mirrored in her eyes. 'When can we expect you?'

'I'll go out with you, Mrs Gray – as soon as I settle things with Mr Darrett.'

Minutes later, Blake turned in the saddle to give Belle a wave. Then he followed after the buckboard. As Blake rode down the street, he saw young Red dragging his boots down the boardwalk, head hanging dejectedly. Further up the boardwalk stood Laslo Callinan, his face expressionless. Life went on, Blake told himself, predictably for most other people, but damned unpredictably for him.

He ate the dust thrown up by the slow-moving buckboard and felt a sense of freedom when they had the town behind them. Sundown, stepping out briskly, went on with an eagerness that told Blake that the big stallion, like himself, had had his fill of towns for the moment.

The week passed and Jesse rode the range every day with Blake Durant. They worked side by side, Durant advising him how to string wire, hogtie a calf for branding, deepen a run-off from the creek. Despite his mother's reproaches, Jesse was at the barn each morning calling for Blake even before the sun was up. He seemed to grow taller in that one week and Blake could see him beginning to fill out.

But it was in the woman that Blake Durant noticed the greatest change. From the very first morning, she seemed to be brighter, and she moved about her work with more enthusiasm. He and Jesse were away most of every day but when they returned to the ranch house, usually dead on sundown, she was there to greet them, showing almost as much welcome for Blake as for her son. Each night Durant retired to the barn loft, where a comfortable bunk had been erected for him and clean sheets laid out. No day passed without something being added to his room, to make it more comfortable for him. So he did his work and taught the boy, and kept a respectable distance from the widow without making it obvious. After seven days he felt as if he was back home, riding the range with his brother.

On the seventh night of his stay and the fifth of harsh dry winds, he washed for supper and headed for the house with the intention of putting their partnership, as she had called it, on a firmer footing. There had been no sign of Slater, Cowley or any of the Box C hands.

Entering the ranch house after knocking lightly on the open door, Blake found Jesse standing in the middle of the main room holding the rifle to his shoulder. His mother was at the stove, her face clouded.

Jesse said, 'I just asked ma, Mr Durant, and she said maybe it was all right by her if you was agreeable.'

'Agreeable to what, Jesse?'

'Well, to learnin' like you, how to handle a gun, Mr Durant. Hell, you know what I was like last time . . . you even made me hand over the rifle less'n I got myself hurt. Well, like I just said to ma, a rancher's got to know how to use a gun.'

Durant remembered how, when he was Jesse's age, his father had thrown him a gun and told him to learn how to use it. He had gone off on his own, chest bursting with pride. In his young mind, the rifle was proof that his father considered him to be on the threshold of manhood. To a boy, that mattered.

'He said, 'How old are you, Jesse?'

'Sixteen.'

'Rising sixteen,' Mrs Gray corrected.

'Hell, I'm so close to sixteen it don't hardly matter,' Jesse threw in.

'It matters a great deal,' Jessica Gray said. 'I don't

want you growing up before your time, son. Now put this gun business out of your head for a moment and sit down to dinner. Have you washed your hands?'

Jesse reluctantly put down the rifle. Then he rushed outside. In a few minutes he was back, on the run, eyes gleaming. When his mother put his dinner before him, he looked eagerly at Blake.

'Will you, Mr Durant?'

Blake saw Jessica Gray's mouth tighten. But there was also resigned acceptance in her face.

He said, 'After the weekend, son. We've got the bottom fence to fix and plenty of wood to put by for winter.'

'Monday then?'

Durant nodded and started on his meal. There was little talk between the adults but Jesse prattled on about the ranch and gulped through his meal and was chided for his bad manners by his mother. Durant had only got through half of his supper before Jesse asked to be excused. Tired of his prattling, his mother let him go. Jesse scooped up the rifle, called out that he was going to clean and oil it and then he ran off in the direction of the barn.

When her son was out of sight, Jessica Gray apologized to Durant who waved her words away and said:

'He's a boy.'

'Yes, but for how long, Mr Durant?'

'No need for the mister,' Blake said.

She smiled shyly. 'Well, Blake then.' She blushed when she said it, then went on, 'You've been so good to us, and Jesse's real fond of you. He needs a man about – needs the kind of discipline only a man can give him.'

She was relaxed now, as Blake seldom saw her. He found it easier to talk himself. 'Boys have a habit of learning things themselves. He's bright and willing and keen. He'll make it, don't trouble yourself about that.'

'I feel he will now,' she said and her smile was warm and grateful.

She left the table and began to clean the dishes. After finishing his meal, Durant went outside and leaned against the hitch rail.

A light came on in the barn and dusk was settling in quickly. By the time Jessica Gray came out to get a breath of evening air, it was dark. Blake was at the rail, where he spent a short time each evening, looking into the distance as if the emptiness out here held something for him. But now he was working out plans for the ranch and did not hear her come up. She said, close to him:

'What do you think about?'

He turned, accidentally brushing a shoulder lightly against her. She caught her breath but didn't move away.

'I don't think, Jessica,' he said. 'I just look, and remember. We all have things to remember.'

'Yes,' she said, her gaze going past him to the darkness beyond the valley. They stood together, the light from the house fading short of them and the light from the barn not strong enough to reach them. They could hear Jesse whistling, and off in the hills a coyote wailed.

Time stood still for both of them. Then, as Jessica turned and looked straight at him, her lips trembling, Blake Durant felt a stirring that had been locked away too long, deep inside him. Her hand touched his arm and he pulled her gently to him. Jessica's lips settled on his and her body came against him.

For a long moment they clung together before Jessica pulled away, her face flushed.

'I'm sorry, Blake, really sorry.'

'No need to be.'

'I led you into that. I shouldn't have . . . I don't know what got into me.'

'It was honest,' he said.

Her lips were moist and her hands shook a little. Then she looked quickly towards the barn where Jesse's shrill whistling still disturbed the night. She touched her hair, then the ribbon of her blouse and regarded him intently for a moment before, with a sudden turn, she hurried towards the house.

Blake Durant stood in the darkness, still feeling the responsive softness of her lips on his. Then he walked to the barn and watched Jesse working on the gun.

'In the morning I'll start teaching you about guns,' Blake said suddenly.

Jesse looked up, eyes wide with disbelief. 'For certain, Mr Durant?'

'Yeah. Best turn in. It's late.'

Jesse grinned. 'Yes, sure, Mr Durant. First thing in the morning!' He called his goodnight on the run and tore down the clearing.

Durant saw the house door open and close and then deeper darkness settled on the clearing. He picked up the lantern and climbed to the loft. As soon as he had his bearings he blew out the light, kicked off his boots and stretched out on the bunk. He lay there blanking his mind against the present and the past and thinking only of the future.

Back at the house, Jesse broke into his mother's thoughtful silence. 'Ma, Mr Durant changed his mind! He's gonna teach me about guns tomorrow, first thing.'

Jessica looked at him for a moment, then placed her hands behind his head and drew him down to her bosom. Despite the feeling that real men didn't allow this, Jesse was too thrilled with the prospect of tomorrow to draw away. Jessica patted his head for a moment, then said:

'Go to bed, son.'

Jesse stepped back from her, frowning because he detected a troubled note in her voice. 'You all right, Ma? You ain't sick or nothin'?'

She smiled faintly. 'No, Jesse, I'm fine. I'm really all right.'

'Well, OK then,' he said and made his way up to his room, where he wondered about grownups who could be as happy as hell and the next minute be all caught up in some worry which wasn't there earlier. He decided that this even happened sometimes to Mr Durant, though not often. He took off his clothes, put on his pajamas and tumbled into bed. As he drew the sheets up to his neck, he smiled.

By hell, after tomorrow he'd stand alongside Mr Durant and help him against the likes of Cowley and Slater. It did not enter Jesse Gray's mind that one day Blake Durant would not be there. It just seemed natural that he always would be.

Downstairs Jessica Gray sighed heavily and wondered how long it would be now before Blake Durant left. Tonight her lack of control had put a barrier between them which neither of them could ignore.

She liked this man, admired him, respected him. But he was not Chad Gray. He was just a stranger who had come along the trail and helped them. She rose, confused still and remembering his tenderness and how he'd neither denied her nor encouraged her. Going to her room, she promised herself it would not happen again, ever.

But later, lying in bed, she touched at her lips and warmth moved through her. She felt suddenly unknotted, loose, released from a tension she realized had been of her own making.

EIGHT

GUNSMOKE TALK

They left their horses on the rim of the slope and made their way down to a shaded valley. Suddenly Durant stopped Jesse by pulling at his arm. Jesse looked curiously at this big man who, every day, managed to surprise him in some way.

'Never walk on the warm side of a rock when the day's cool, Jesse. When it's hot never walk on the cool side.'

Jesse frowned at him, unable to get the gist of this.

'Rattlers like their comforts, too,' Durant told him and went on past the shaded side of the big rock.

Jesse looked at the sun on the ground and shrugged. He had no mind for nature lessons today, only gun-play and things like that. They walked on

126

for another hundred yards before Durant picked out a place where there was both sunlight and shade and a boulder sitting squat, as it had for centuries, dead ahead.

Durant pointed. 'Put the can there, boy.'

Jesse hurried off, put the preserve can on the boulder and ran back. He was more excited than he'd ever been. Durant handed him his own six-gun, saying:

'A handgun is most likely to serve you best since you can carry it into most trouble-spots. Get the feel of it.'

Jesse took the gun and balanced it in his palm. It seemed immensely heavy to him. But after a few moments he nodded, saying, 'Okay, I got the feel of it, Mr Durant.'

Durant had settled down on a tree stump and was making himself a cigarette. He did not look up when the boy spoke.

'To get the proper feel of a gun, boy, you've got to wait until it's like a part of your hand, an extension to it. When you draw, it nestles into your palm as if it belongs there.'

Jesse kept changing the gun from hand to hand and after a while he said, 'Hell, it's right. It gets to feel more and more comfortable.'

'If it doesn't feel comfortable, never pick it up,'

Durant said. He rose, took the gun from Jesse, aimed it at the can and squeezed the trigger. Jesse braced himself for the roar of the shot but no sound came, only a dead clack as the hammer hit home on an empty chamber.

His face darkened and he frowned at Durant who handed the gun back. 'Try it.'

'But, hell, how'll I know how I'm doin' with no bullets?'

'I'll know,' Durant said.

Jesse aimed and triggered, aimed and triggered again. He then turned to the tall man and said, 'Ain't nothin' to this.'

Durant gave him a wry smile. 'The way you jerk your hand up, those bullets might've knocked down a buzzard, but nothing else. Just stretch the hand and tighten on the trigger, easing it back. Never take your eyes off what you're shooting at.'

Jesse went through the motions unhappily. Durant kept him at it for a long time until the boy's arm ached from holding the gun out.

'What's the use of all this?' Jesse grumbled. 'You got to get the gun out first before you can fire it. Teach me to draw.'

Durant shook his head. 'What's the use of drawing a gun if you don't know how to fire it? First things first. Tired?'

128

'Some,' said Jesse, rubbing his aching forearm.

'Then we're through for the day. Tomorrow it'll be easier.'

Durant prodded out bullets from his belt and filled his gun. Jesse stood close to him and pointed to the can. 'How's about hittin' it for me?'

Durant holstered the gun. As he walked away, he said, 'A can never hurt anybody. Come on, boy. Work to be done.'

They didn't speak more than a dozen words to each other all day and when Jesse arrived back at the ranch house he quickly unsaddled his horse and made his way to his mother.

When she greeted him enthusiastically, he said: 'Some teacher,' and went on to his room.

Jessica watched him go off, then turned to see Blake Durant walking into the barn. She felt a rise of uneasiness inside her at the sight of him and dreaded mealtime with all the remembering and embarrassment. She continued to prepare the meal, wearing an old frock that she knew had long since ceased to flatter her. When Blake Durant appeared at the doorway, washed and in a change of clothes, she felt a kind of chill go through her.

He said, 'We made good progress with the gun.'

'I'm glad,' she said and fussed about the stove, her back to him.

'Come a week or so, he'll make out well enough. Then all he'll have to do is practice and remember.'

Jesse's door opened as Blake spoke. There was a hint of curiosity in the boy's face.

'In a week . . . all that time?' he asked.

'A man can get killed in a second, Jesse,' Durant told him and took his seat at the table.

While the meal progressed he kept his eyes on his food, aware of the tension in the woman and pained because of it. But as soon as he finished his meal, he sat back, wiped his hands and mouth on a table napkin and said:

'Time we thought about stocking up the place.'

Jessica gaped at him. 'Stock? But how? We can't afford to buy anything. We're lucky enough now just to make ends meet and—'

'A place is no good without stock. Stock multiply themselves. Start with fifty cows and a bull and in three years' time you've got a few hundred. Only way.'

Jesse was looking as shocked as his mother. 'You mean you're going to buy cows for us?'

'For all of us,' Durant said. 'I've invested money in the place and I don't want to see it go to waste. In time you'll pay me back.'

Jessica's face was filled with emotion. She shook her head, the lantern light catching at the loose curls of her hair. 'We can't let you,' she said.

'You can't stop me, ma'am,' Durant said. He got to his feet and ruffled Jesse's hair. 'Be earlier tomorrow.'

With that he went out. Jessica and the boy sat at the table and Jesse said, 'Gosh, Ma, cows and everything.'

She nodded, not daring to say a word, full of happiness for the first time in years.

Later she looked at herself in the mirror in her room and tore her old frock off, swearing she would never wear it again except for some chore for which it was fitted.

That night she lay down and remembered what a preacher had told her when she was a lot younger:

'Girl, the wind blows into your face and chokes and blinds you one day, and the next it blows from behind, helping you along. Be patient and good times will follow the bad.'

Well, she told herself, she had been patient. She had done the best she could and learned to live with her fears. Now she wondered if the wind was really beginning to blow from the other direction and if, somehow, miraculously, she would soon be able to give Jesse some of the things he needed and wanted, and if there might not be enough left over for the necessary things she herself needed. She closed her eyes and tried not to think of anything, believing that if she did, she would make all the promise disappear, never to be regained.

Griff Darrett walked into the saloon ten days after he had talked with Blake Durant in his office at the bank. He looked troubled so Belle went to him, saying:

'You look like somebody just robbed your bank, Griff.'

Jolted out of his thoughts, Griff Darrett gave her a guarded smile. 'No, not as bad as that, Belle.'

'Nothing I can do to help?'

Darrett looked over her full, rounded body and then into her attractive face. He had never been able to understand Belle Hudson. She pretended to be so damned hard, always holding herself in rigid reserve, yet underneath he sensed there was more tenderness in her than most women would know in a lifetime. He had seen her help out drunks, give handouts to old-timers, assist people in a number of ways. Happily married himself, with four fine boys and a daughter, he could not understand how people like Belle got on without the joys of such a union.

'I'm just waiting for Tom Dowd,' he said.

At that moment Marie walked up, breathed a sigh of boredom, acknowledged Darrett's cursory look and sat beside Belle.

'I'm going out to see Gus Cowley,' Darrett went on. 'There's some hard business to get settled, an option to hand back. Cowley isn't going to be in the best of tempers when he hears about it, so I'm taking Tom along.'

Belle looked thoughtful. 'Has this something to do with the Gray place?'

Marie was suddenly all attention.

Darrett nodded. 'Yes. That stranger who happened by a week or so ago rocked me right back on my heels the other day when he paid up the mortgage on the Gray place. I don't rightly understand his reasons, but what he did has enabled that woman and her boy to keep the place. Which means Cowley is going to hit the sky.'

Marie, shifting forward to study Darrett more intently, said, 'You don't mean to say, Mr Darrett, that Mr Durant has taken up with the Gray woman, do you? Why, she isn't any more than a worn-out, plain old—'

'Marie!' Belle cut in angrily. 'Go and help out back and keep your silly little thoughts to yourself.'

Marie straightened on the seat, aghast at the bitterness in Belle's voice. Her mouth remained open even when she left the stool. Another severe look from Belle sent her scuttling away. As soon as Marie

had gone, Belle regained her composure and asked:
'Is it that way, Griff?'

Darrett pretended not to understand the question
so Belle expanded. 'Jessica Gray and Durant? Have
they taken up with each other?'

Darrett was clearly disturbed by so blunt a question. 'Hell, I don't know, Belle. Durant's a peculiar
kind of jasper from what I've seen and heard of him.
Who knows what a man like that has in mind? But I
don't go along with Marie. I think Jessica Gray is one
of the finest women I've ever known. After that terrible accident to her husband, Chad, I squirm when I
think how little I could do to help her. There could
be something between them, but I'm saying only that
Durant's out there, whipping the place into shape.
He's got some kind of partnership going with the
Grays.'

Belle breathed a deep sigh and called for a drink
from Hap. Since it was still early morning, Darrett
was mildly surprised. Belle rarely had a drink before
late afternoon, reserving herself for late at night
when she often sat with businessmen and discussed
Crimson Falls' future.

A difficult silence settled, with Griff Darrett
remembering details of Belle's association with
Durant which were widely discussed in town. He had
a second drink before Tom Dowd showed up. The

sheriff, after acknowledging Belle's presence, said curtly:

'Okay, Griff, let's get it over with.'

Darrett swung off the stool and nodded at Belle. Wearing a still-troubled look, he made his way to the batwing doors. But Belle detained Dowd by grasping his wrist.

'Will you be going through the Gray place, Tom?'

Dowd shrugged. 'No need to. I'll have enough trouble with Cowley, I reckon.'

'I just thought ... if you happen to see Blake Durant, you might give him my regards.'

Dowd studied her face. 'Cowley will be enough for me, today, Belle. I sure don't hanker to fit Durant in, too. This damn town is beginning to figure me for a damn diplomat.'

'Don't worry then,' Belle said and walked away, shoulders squared and head lifted.

Dowd joined Darrett on the boardwalk where both their horses were waiting. In the saddle, Dowd took a careful look up and down the street and found it quiet. Satisfied that the town could look after itself for a few hours, he sent his horse running, but not before saying to Griff Darrett:

'If Cowley bucks, let me handle it. And I mean that, Griff. Cowley, I don't have to tell you, has big ideas on himself.'

'You don't have to tell anybody in this town that, Tom. Look, after I hand him back his option, I'm finished with him. And I don't like to do it, not with him such a good customer of the bank. But what could I do? Durant settled the matter legally and it's out of my hands.'

They rode out of town. With Tom Dowd setting a fast pace, they crossed Dry Plains and made their way into the foothills. Dowd seemed completely unaffected by the heat but Darrett called for a rest before they had gone ten miles. Sitting his horse in timber shade, he mopped his brow and muttered:

'Now you tell me, Tom, just what the hell do those range men get out of this damned country? Dust and heat and damn flies and a sore seat. It don't appeal to me one bit.'

'Try putting them in your office, confined, stale air, same surroundings, and they'd go berserk, Griff. It's not far now.'

Darrett moved his sore bottom in the saddle and sighed in resignation. Then he trailed Dowd across another run of hills until finally they reached Cowley country. The hot sun burned relentlessly down. Dust billowed with the wind and Darrett found himself hardly able to breathe. But once in the shade of the Box C ranch house porch, he began to feel better.

Gus Cowley came onto the porch, studying them

grimly at first, squinting to get his eyes used to the sun-glare. When he recognized Griff Darrett, his face brightened.

'Well, howdy, Darrett, Dowd. Damn near forgot what day it was, been too damn busy herdin' cows. Come in, come in, have a drink, sit down and enjoy the cool.'

Darrett looked nervously at Dowd, drew in a deep breath and let Dowd precede him onto the porch. He looked about the heat-seared, dust-choked clearing and wondered how anybody could live in such circumstances. Inside, he found Jud Slater leaning against the living room wall. Cowley fussed about at his whisky cabinet and Dowd stood in the center of the room, his face expressionless as he took in Jud Slater, whose right arm still carried a bandage.

Cowley came back with drinks, took their hats, tossed them onto a divan and pointed to chairs. 'Relax, make yourselves at home. Good day this, one I've been waiting for for a long time. It couldn't come soon enough for me.'

Darrett drew papers from his pocket, leaving his drink untasted. He stole a look at Tom Dowd, settled on the divan, then Darrett drove his long legs out and made himself comfortable.

Cowley was in high spirits. But Griff Darrett, feeling that a devil was on his shoulder, suddenly cleared his throat and said:

'Mr Cowley, there's something you should know right away.'

'Sure is, Griff. How much I got to pay? Don't really matter how much, but don't try to cheat me blind. Still, I'm willing to give a point or two for the help you gave me. What is it? A thousand, fifteen hundred?'

Darrett looked at Dowd who completely ignored him. The banker said, 'No money is going to change hands, Mr Cowley. You see, there's been a change in things.'

Cowley spun on him, his face darkening. 'No money? How come?'

'The Gray place ain't for sale any longer.'

Cowley straightened, his hand tightening on his glass. 'What do you mean it ain't for sale? I got an option on it! The mortgage falls due today and I'm picking up my option. So cut the foolery, mister, and state the amount. I'll give you my note, sign some papers and the deal's finished.'

Darrett gulped. 'There'll be no signing,' he said.

Slater shifted away from the wall and worked his fingers. But Cowley gave him a warning look and strode across to Darrett. His face was livid with rage now.

'Plainer, mister, real plain, straight down the line!'

Darrett wiped sweat from his forehead. He had never known a hotter day. 'The mortgage was met,' he said.

A curse exploded from Cowley. 'Met? What the hell are you talking about? That widow hasn't got a dime to bless herself with. She ain't got nothing to sell up either. She's down, finished!'

'Just the same,' Cowley said, 'the mortgage was met.'

'By your stinkin' bank, Darrett?' Cowley barked. 'You give her a damn extension?'

Darrett shook his head. 'No, there was no extension. There was no need for one. The mortgage was paid up, to the cent. She's free to work her place for as long as she likes and nobody can shift her off.'

'As plain as that,' Dowd put in, rising to his feet and regarding Slater contemptuously.

Griff Darrett knew of Slater's prowess with a gun and was surprised to see Dowd so disdainful, of the gun-handler.

Cowley spun on the lawman. 'Keep out of this, Dowd. This is between me and this snivellin' bank clerk.'

'I'm here to see the law upheld and no trouble made, Cowley. Darrett's stated his case.'

'To hell he has!' Cowley roared. 'You figure me to take this lying down? That damn widow didn't have a cent, nothing. So how come the mortgage was paid up? How come—' He stopped in mid-sentence and eyed Darrett malevolently. 'Who?' he demanded. 'Give the person a name!'

Darrett swallowed hard. This was the moment he'd been fearing. Cowley took him by the shoulder and turned him against the wall. But Dowd was quick to reach them and he plucked Cowley's hand away. He stood gravely before Cowley.

'Who, damn you?' Cowley demanded of Darrett.

Darrett worked away from Cowley and glanced at Dowd who calmly nodded his head.

Darrett cleared his throat and muttered, 'Blake Durant!'

Cowley, struck speechless, stepped away from the banker, his face losing color. Then he looked meaningfully at Jud Slater and saw the fierce anger in the gunfighter's face.

'Durant!'

The word was like a curse from Cowley's tight-lipped mouth. 'Durant!' he said again. He walked away from Darrett and Dowd, his shoulders slumped.

Darrett said, 'Blake Durant came to see me and paid over the money owed on the mortgage.'

Cowley moved restlessly about the room for some time before he turned suddenly to Darrett again. He mouthed a curse and backhanded the banker in the face. Then he made to hit the stumbling banker again, but Dowd grabbed his shoulder and hurled him away. Dowd's hand dived down for his gun but before he could clear leather, Jud Slater had his gun trained on him.

'Don't, lawman!' Slater snapped.

Dowd's hand froze. His eyes filled with hostility. Then Darrett regained his balance and turned on Cowley.

'Damn you! Can't you ever see another man's point of view.'

Slater stood with the gun leveled on Dowd as Cowley stepped back, a nerve working at his temple. In that moment, Griff Darrett knew that Slater, given the order by Cowley, would surely kill. It was there in Slater's face – complete contempt for the law and everything Dowd stood for. There was also a depth of viciousness in Slater's black eyes that proclaimed him a killer.

'Don't be a fool, Cowley,' Darrett told the rancher.

Cowley's chest heaved under the strain of his fury. Then he said, 'Get out, Dowd, and take this snivellin' scum with you. Get to hell off my place and don't ever come back.'

Dowd lifted his hand from his gun butt and nodded for Darrett to move. The banker was only too willing. He hurried to the door and, without looking back, made for his horse. Following him, Sheriff Tom Dowd said:

'Take it easy, Cowley. You're not a law unto your-self in these parts. You worry the hell out of that widow and her boy, and by hell I'll come after you.'

'Just git while you got the means to do it, mister,' snapped Cowley and he motioned for Slater to put up his gun. He stood in the middle of the living room, his face burning, his lips white and tightly compressed and his hands clenched. When the sound of hoof beats sounded outside he said:

'Durant! By hell, I'll get him!'

NINE

A LONER'S FURY

Sheriff Dowd forced Darrett to go with him to the Gray ranch. There they found Jessica Gray on her own. Durant and Jesse had already left for the bottom country where Blake Durant meant to bargain for some good stock for the place. Dowd told Jessica that Cowley was making threats and thought he would hunt down Durant. He left word for Durant to be on his guard. Unable to be of further help, he continued on to town, dragging a crushed Darrett with him. In all his dealings with hard and vicious men, Griff Darrett couldn't remember a man who had frightened him as much as Gus Cowley had. In town, he went straight to his bank and locked himself in his office. Only then, when he had the familiar drab walls, the old solid furniture and the sounds of business around him, did he relax to any degree.

Dowd left his horse outside the jailhouse, returned down the street to the saloon, and had more drinks than he had ever had in a full week. He had the uncomfortable feeling that there was more he should be doing about this trouble, but he couldn't see how. Although Dowd's sympathies were with the widow and her son, he felt that Durant had made his play and had to see it through. Later, Dowd would pick up the pieces.

Blake Durant visited three ranches in the bottom country below the Gray place before he found the stock he was looking for. He herded off fifty head of good prime cattle for a price he felt was fair. Turning them back home, he watched the excitement rise in Jesse's face and for the first time in many months felt the thrill of accomplishment take hold.

It was a hot day and the air was still, broken only by the rumble of the cattle across the dry-grass country. At the Gray place he saw Jessica waiting at the door of the house, her apron flapping in the breeze, her hair tidy, looking as fresh as the valley country they had just come from. Jesse rode ahead, reined in near his mother and pointed at the herd.

He did not say anything – his beaming face said all that needed to be said.

Jessica, surprisingly to Blake Durant, did not show any enthusiasm over the arrival of the cattle. He worked the herd towards the yards, then came back to her. Jesse rode off, eager to get back to the cattle and start the branding Durant had promised would take place as soon as possible.

Jessica frowned at Durant and said, 'Gus Cowley happened by. Before that I had a visit from Sheriff Dowd and the banker, Griff Darrett.'

'So?' Durant said.

'Tom Dowd said he'd just told Cowley that he couldn't take over this place. They were gone no more than twenty minutes when Cowley came by, cursing and ranting and demanding to know where you were. He had seven men with him, including Jud Slater.'

Durant nodded. 'Where'd they head?'

'I told them nothing, Blake,' she said. 'They could-n't get a word out of me.'

It was then that he noticed a welt on the side of her cheek.

'Who hit you, Jessica?' he demanded.

'Slater,' she said.

'Where'd they go?'

'Towards town.'

'How long ago?'

She licked her lips and moved closer to him, shaking her head. 'No, Blake. Let them curse and abuse us, but don't fight them. There's no need for fight.'

'How long ago?' he asked again and her shoulders slumped.

'An hour. They'll be halfway to town by now.'

'Which way?'

'Down the valley.'

He straightened in the saddle and looked across to where Jesse was climbing the yard rails. 'Look after the boy,' he said, then he wheeled Sundown around and cut him into a run.

The thunder of his going forced Jessica to let out a cry which she immediately choked back. Tears formed in her eyes and her face was ashen with anxiety. Jesse came running to her a moment later and looked at the cloud of dust raised by Sundown.

'Where's Mr Durant gone, Ma?'

'To town, Jesse.'

'Now, this late?'

'He has some business to attend to. It has nothing to do with us, so wash up and we'll have an early supper.'

Jesse pulled away from her. 'But, Ma, there's the cattle to brand. Mr Durant said—'

Her stern look took the boy by surprise. Then, as he saw tears building up in her eyes, he bit back his protest and walked away, looking back often before he reached the trough at the side of the house. Jessica Gray, standing rigidly, wrung her hands in desperation. She did not move until Durant was out of sight.

Sheriff Tom Dowd saw Durant ride down the street just on sundown. He locked up his jailhouse, hurried into the street and intercepted Durant.

'Where are they, Sheriff?' Blake said.

Dowd shook his head slowly. 'There are too many for you, Durant. Best ride out.'

Durant gave no answer. He turned at a noise from Belle Hudson's saloon, then let Sundown walk on. Dowd walked quickly along at his side, keeping pace, watching Durant's cold eyes taking stock of the street.

'Damn you, Durant, you're no match for that lot. There's seven of them, part drunk. My guess is they're getting up steam to pay you a visit tonight.'

'No need for them to wait,' Durant said and rode on. Dowd cursed him and Durant said, 'Dowd, you're a good lawman. Keep out of this, for the town's sake.'

'Maybe I can stop it,' Dowd muttered.

Durant gave him a thin smile. 'No. Cowley's called the tune.'

Dowd wiped his face hard and rubbed sweat from his palms. More noise rose from the saloon. Down the boardwalks people knotted together, plainly worried about the saloon ruckus. More than one person hurried home. Blake Durant came out of the saddle before the saloon, listened a moment, then walked straight for the batwing doors. Dowd was only a few paces behind him.

Durant pushed aside the doors and entered the saloon. The noise rose tumultuously about him as he walked to the bar. Gus Cowley stood at the counter, scowling into his drink. Jud Slater was standing a short distance away, no glass in his hand, his face hooded in thought. The other hands, including Arch Briller, were drinking heavily and making a lot of noise. Belle and Marie were at the top of the stairs, both looking worried. Hap, sweating, was trying without success to control the boisterous, jostling Cowley hands.

Tom Dowd worked his way along the wall. He sighted Belle and nodded; then, as she started to come down the stairs, he pushed his way through the crowd towards her, catching the attention of Slater and Cowley. During this distraction, Blake Durant crossed unseen to the counter and signaled Hap towards him. Hap gaped, stole a look Cowley's way and hurried to Blake.

Durant ordered a whisky, paid for it, drank it down, then stepped away from the counter. He stood casually, looking straight down the bar at the Box C crowd. Men nearby studied him and moved off. This allowed Durant a better view of Slater and Gus Cowley.

He said, 'Looking for me, Cowley?'

Cowley spun about, his glass cracking against the counter's edge.

'Durant!' he snarled.

'Your move,' Durant said.

Cowley pushed a hired hand aside and moved away from the counter. A moment's indecision showed in his face, then his lips peeled back in a snarl. Suddenly his hand flashed for his gun. But, as he drew, Jud Slater hurled him aside. Durant's gun came out with a blur and bucked in his hand. His bullet took Cowley in the shoulder and sent him reeling. Then Durant's cold eyes bored at Slater who'd been outdrawn.

At the bottom of the stairs, Tom Dowd said, 'You want me to stop it, Belle?'

Belle shook her head. 'No, Tom. It has to be. They both know it. It's here or someplace else, some other time.'

Cowley had regained his feet, but his gun had been jolted from his grip. Directly behind him Arch

Briller shifted to keep Cowley between Durant and himself. The other hands backed away under the sweep of Blake Durant's fierce stare. Slater's hand stayed fixed on his gun butt.

Blake Durant said, 'We'll finish it now, Slater.'

Men moved away from Slater. Dowd, easing Belle aside, walked forward, checking off the Cowley hands. Gus Cowley shouted wild curses and charged at Durant. But Blake, hardly looking at him, swung his gun and smashed Cowley down.

Slater made another move for his gun but Durant's Peacemaker was leveled at him. Slater lifted his hand but Durant knew that, given a chance, Slater would shoot him down.

He decided to give him that chance. He stepped further away from the counter and said, 'Tom, watch the others.'

Then he planted his feet wide and slowly let his gun drop into his holster. Slater's mouth twitched and vicious hatred burned from his eyes.

'You call,' Durant said.

Slater worked his shoulders and glanced to where Cowley lay still. Then his hand went down. His gun cleared leather with a speed that brought a gasp from Belle. For a brief moment grim satisfaction showed in Slater's eyes. Durant had not seemed to move except to lower his left shoulder. But the

Peacemaker was in his hand, bucking.

The bullets tore into Slater, sending him rocking back to the bar. Cowley looked up from the floor to see Slater going down. All color left the rancher's face. The other Box C men backed off as if the bullets were ripping into them. Not one of them went for his gun.

Blake Durant stood still, cordite smoke rising to veil his features. There was no emotion in his face. His eyes were vacant. Then the tension went out of Durant and he looked at Tom Dowd. Dowd nodded and drew his own gun, saying:

'It's finished. That's it.'

Cowley, helped to his feet, stared at Blake Durant. Blood streamed down the side of his face and from his shoulder. Arch Briller was the first of the Box C men to speak:

'I'm cutting out, Durant. I want no part of you.'

Durant's look touched on Briller. 'Ride.'

Briller looked at his companions. One by one they edged past Cowley.

'Where the hell are you going?' Cowley barked.

Nobody answered. When they were gone, he looked down at the motionless Jud Slater and his shoulders slumped.

'Damn you, Durant!' he croaked and then he turned and went out to the boardwalk. Durant

151

picked up Slater's gun, followed Cowley out, swung onto Sundown and rode from town.

Jessica Gray stood on the porch. Jesse was in bed. He'd insisted on staying up with his mother to await Blake Durant's return. But the hard work on the spread had fatigued the youngster, and he'd fallen asleep on the sofa. He was too heavy for Jessica to carry, so she'd walked him into his bedroom. Jesse was so weary that he wasn't aware he was on his feet . . .

It was late. The spread was a long way from town, but Durant should have been here by now. He would come, she told herself, refusing to believe that anything could stop him, not Cowley or Slater or all the hands from the Box C. But then she thought of the death she'd seen in Slater's eyes. Slater was a man who lived by the gun. Durant was no killer. Oh, he'd killed, but only because he'd been forced to.

And there was Cowley. He hated Durant for paying the note on the spread. Cowley was no ordinary man. He was polite enough, even affable, when things were going his way, but he was a vicious enemy. How far was Cowley prepared to go to exact vengeance on Blake Durant? Sheriff Dowd would be no help; she'd sensed this when Dowd came to the house with Griff Darrett. Dowd wasn't on Cowley's side, but he was just one man.

Something caught her eye. A falling star! The last time she'd seen one she hadn't made a wish. Now she did. She closed her eyes and in her mind she said: 'Protect him. Save him. Don't let him die . . .'

Then she listened to the silence of the night, not opening her eyes, holding onto the wish. She stood there, an arm around a porch post. Finally her arm felt numb and it was a great strain to keep her eyelids down. But she didn't want to open her eyes, didn't want to see the empty darkness.

Then she heard it. At first she thought it was her imagination manufacturing the sound, or that maybe she was hearing the throbbing of the nerves that pulsed at her temples. She keened her ears and the sound grew louder . . . the drumming of hoofs. When she was absolutely certain that a horse was approaching, she opened her eyes.

The hoof beats grew louder and louder. She peered into the darkness. Any moment now she would see the horse and rider. There – a moving shadow in the darkness.

'Let it be him, oh Lord! Let it be him!'

Then:

'Blake! Oh, Blake!'

She ran down the steps towards Durant. He reined in Sundown and leaped from the saddle. She stopped when she was a few paces away.

'It is you,' she breathed.

The long ride had accustomed his eyes to the darkness and he could see her pale face clearly. There was the shine of a tear on her cheek.

'Cowley?' she said.

He nodded. 'I saw him. And Slater. It's all over, Jessica.'

She grasped his arm. 'Are you. . . ?'

'I'm fine.'

She started to lower her head so he wouldn't see the tears, but he reached out and lifted her chin with a gentle hand.

'Please,' she said, 'I'm making a fool of myself.'

'Never be ashamed of tears, Jessica.'

Then she was in his arms and his lips were on hers. She opened her mouth to his kiss and pressed herself hard against his body. But then her hands were on his chest and she pushed him away. He let his hands drop to his sides.

'It's late,' he said, and there was a tremor in his voice. 'You go to bed. I'll take care of Sundown and—'

'I'll be waiting for you in the barn,' she said. Before he could speak, she turned and walked across the clearing.

Durant watched her disappear through the doorway of the barn. She'd lost control of herself for a moment and wanted to get her composure back, he thought. She probably wanted to talk to him about future plans, and maybe she was anxious to know what had happened in Crimson Falls.

He unsaddled Sundown, then walked him around to cool him off before taking him to the water trough. After that he took a rough towel from his saddle-bag and dried the perspiration flecks from the horse's black hide. He walked Sundown into the barn and looked around but he didn't see Jessica. He made sure the horse's water pail was full and he left Sundown munching oats in his stall.

'Blake . . .'

Jessica's voice came from the darkness at the end of the barn. He walked there and she stepped out of the shadows. He sucked in his breath at the perfection of her naked body.

'Love me,' she whispered.

He started to reach for her, stopped his hands. 'The boy,' he said.

'He's in the house, asleep. Don't you want me, Blake?'

'I sure do, Jessica.'

'Then come and take me.'

But he hesitated. 'This – this might be just a reaction,' he mumbled. 'You're glad I wasn't hurt and . . . and . . .'

155

Her teeth flashed in the darkness. 'You're very good at thinking up excuses, aren't you?'

'Jessica . . .'

They moved forward at the same time. His hands glided down her shoulders and over the curve of her back. She turned her face up to him, her lips parted. It was a sweet, gentle kiss at first, then their yearning for each other became a savage pounding, a demand that couldn't be denied. She leaned back and a long, deep sigh came from her.

'Oh, darling . . . Oh, darling . . .'

She went limp in his arms. He lifted her from the floor and carried her across the barn to his bed . . .

They lay back, breathing easily, passions spent.

'Sleep,' she said.

'Jesse . . . he might wake up and find us here.'

'I'll awake before he will. I always do. Sleep, Blake. I want to feel you beside me for a while . . . I'll go to the house before dawn.'

He closed his eyes and sleep came almost immediately.

But Jessica lay awake, content to feel her flesh against his, to hear his level breathing. After a while Durant began to dream, and then he whispered a name.

'Louise . . .'

156

There was tenderness in his voice. But suddenly his body jerked.

'Louise!'

There was anguish now.

'Louise! Louise!'

'It's all right,' Jessica said soothingly, her hand caressing his cheek. 'Easy, Blake, easy.'

His body stopped jerking. It was as though he heard her voice and was taking comfort from her nearness.

She stayed beside him until she was sure the dream had ended, then she eased herself away, put her clothes on quickly and walked to the house.

Now she knew what had made Blake Durant the man he was. And she also knew that she couldn't take the place of Louise, nor could any other woman. Later, maybe, but not now . . .

Jesse was overjoyed to see Durant in the barn the next morning. His mother had told him to go out to the barn and the youngster ran all the way.

No work was done for most of that morning. Durant had to tell Jesse exactly what had happened in town, move for move, over and over again. Jessica Gray stood in the background while they spoke, a gentle smile on her lips. Finally Durant sent Jesse to his room to get rigged up for work. He turned to Jessica, licked at his lips.

'I don't think I can say how much last night meant to me,' he said. 'But—'

'Don't,' she said, knowing that he was going to tell her about Louise. 'Look, Blake, I think we should both do our best to forget about last night.'

He looked surprised. She turned away and said:

'I like you, in fact I'm very fond of you, but we're just not right for each other. I have my life to lead and you have yours, and we're going in opposite directions.' She looked into his eyes. 'Do you understand, Blake?'

He smiled. 'I understand only one thing – you're too good for me.'

She felt tears coming and had to turn away again. Love for him filled her being, but she couldn't let him know. He'd already had tragedy in his life; it would be cruel to make him feel shame and remorse. She had to do all in her power to make the parting easy for him. And the day of parting would come; it had to; Blake Durant was a man who needed change – new faces, new surroundings. It was necessary for him to keep on the move, ever searching. Someday he would find himself, would be able to pick up the threads of day-to-day life and settle down. Maybe he would select her. If so, she would be waiting. She'd make sure he knew that before he left; she'd find ways to tell him.

Durant slapped the boy on the back. 'All right, partner, let's be on the move.'

Jessica watched them go. Not until they were on their horses and riding away did she let the tears come.

For two days they roped and branded the cattle, Jessica insisting that the new brand be D bar G. Durant offered no argument. When the cattle were turned into the valley, Durant and Jesse returned to the barn. After supper, Durant told Jesse to practice with the gun he had picked up from the floor of the saloon near Jud Slater's bullet-riddled body.

To Jessica Gray he said, 'Nobody will trouble you again.'

In the morning Jesse ran back to the house from the barn and called:

'Ma, Mr Durant ain't at the barn. Bed's rolled up and his horse is gone.'

Jessica felt sharp pain dig into her bosom. She caught at her throat with shaking fingers. Jesse stood back, looking tearfully at her.

'He's gone, Ma?' he asked, choking on the words.

Jessica could do no more than nod. She caught her son to her and hugged him desperately, as if he, too, might suddenly be lost to her.

'Why, Ma, why? Didn't he like it here?'

'He liked it fine, Jesse. He liked us very much. But

Mr Durant is his own kind of man and he must do what he must.'

Jesse pulled clear. 'Will he come back, Ma? Will be ever?'

Jessica wiped the tears from her cheeks and showed a brave look to Jesse. 'Maybe,' she said. Then she managed a smile, even though the loss of Blake Durant was crushing the feelings out of her.

'One day, Jesse,' she said, 'he may come riding over the ridge and everything will be fine again. But you've got to remember what he taught you so you can look after me. His brand is on the cattle, isn't it?'

'Well, yeah,' Jesse said.

'It's also on us, son.'

'His brand,' Jesse said, and suddenly the boy seemed to grow a little taller. 'Maybe he figures I'm big enough now to look after things, Ma.'

'I'm sure of that,' she said. Then she hurried into the house, not wanting Jesse to see the new tears in her eyes.

She looked at the empty room where her husband had been and where Blake Durant had been. Even if he didn't come back, part of him would be there . . . would always be there . . .